UNFORTUNATE EVENT

Marc David Veldt

ISBN: 1502913402
ISBN 13: 9781502913401
Library of Congress Control Number: 2014918869
CreateSpace Independent Publishing Platform
North Charleston, South Carolina

For PJM, my favorite Canadian

Justice is an essential part of righteousness.
Theodore Roosevelt

Prologue

Jack Andrews watched as Carl Hafen appeared at the restaurant's door, a leggy young woman at his side. Jack knew his money was paying for that particular piece of ass. Hafen turned as he exited, waving to someone inside. A few seconds later lights began going out inside the eating establishment. Carl and his date were the last customers of the night.

The couple walked side by side toward the Mercedes. The woman, tipsy, grabbed Hafen's arm.

Jack Andrews looked around. He saw no one

He pulled a ski mask over his face, stood up, held the .22 pistol against his right thigh, and walked directly to the couple, his head down to avoid eye contact.

The woman saw him at the last moment. Hafen had his back to them, unlocking the passenger side door. In a tight voice the woman said, "Carl, get the door open."

He was next to them. Hafen turned his head to see why his woman was distressed. Jack walked directly to him, pulled the pistol up, and pushed it hard into the center of his target's back. Hafen said, "Wait."

Jack pressed the trigger. The discharge was almost inaudible. Hafen went straight down, his spine shattered at the level of the first lumbar vertebra.

The woman opened her mouth to scream. Jack took a step toward her and backhanded the pistol against her face. She went down without a sound, unconscious.

Jack knelt down next to Hafen. He looked around his perimeter and saw nothing. No one moving, no one talking, no one alarmed. He grabbed his enemy by the shoulders and turned him over. He sat him up against the front tire of the Mercedes. Hafen was awake, his breathing labored. His eyes registered panic.

Jack pushed the muzzle of the pistol into Hafen's sternum, right over his heart. He lifted his ski mask so Hafen could see his face, then pulled it down again. "Remember me, Carl?"

The reply came in a hoarse voice. "Look, we can work this out. Don't do anything else to me. We're even now. I won't tell anyone."

"Gee, Carl, that's hard to believe. I've just killed your girlfriend. Are you just going to let that go too?"

"She's just a toy. There's plenty more like her. I swear I won't tell anyone. Just go away."

Jack looked hard into the stricken man's eyes. "But if you do tell anyone, I'll come back. Understand?" Hafen nodded. "But Carl, I have to know one thing. And if you lie to me I'll become angry. How did you hear about the case you used to ruin me? Who put you on to me?"

"My secretary. Her husband's a janitor at the hospital. He told me about the case."

"And why, of all the doctors involved, was I chosen as the target?"

Choked words hurried out. "He said you had big-time personal problems at home. You were depressed. You'd be easy to break on the stand. I swear it was nothing personal. It was just business."

Jack squeezed the trigger. There was another muffled pop. Carl Hafen's eyes opened wide in surprise. Then all light left them.

CHAPTER ONE

"Hey, Doc, can you take a look at this guy before we send him up to the ward? He just doesn't look right."

Anesthesiologist Jack Andrews had been deep in discussion with neurosurgeon David Kelly, arguing whether the University of Nebraska football team would play for the national championship in seven months, a prospect Dr. Andrews deemed unlikely. This topic ranked just below national security and the state of the economy as a matter of importance in Omaha. Every person in the operating room participated in the discussion.

In no way did the discussion distract anyone from performing his or her individual tasks. It was the interplay common for all people in teamwork situations. A background of meaningless chatter indicated all was going well. The surgical team was half an hour into an operation for the drainage of an epidural hematoma. The patient on the operating room table had fallen off a roof and struck his head. A blood clot formed and was now pressing on his brain. The neurosurgeon was opening the skull to drain the blood.

Though an emergency procedure, it was not technically difficult. Success could be almost guaranteed. The anesthesia machine easily ventilated the patient, vital signs stayed stable, intravenous access remained secure. Jack relaxed. Everything was progressing exactly as it should.

Stan Sanderson, a registered nurse, had left the recovery room and walked directly across the hallway into operating room 3. He wanted to discuss the previous occupant of OR3, a patient who'd spent the last hour and a half emerging from a general anesthetic, an anesthetic administered to him by Jack. Stan was not given to undue pessimism or panic. That he'd taken time to don a surgical cap and mask so he could enter an OR to speak face to face with his supervising physician was out of character. He had Jack's complete attention.

"What could be wrong, Stan? The last patient looked fine before we started this case. He even tried to get me to increase the dosage of morphine I ordered. He tried to convince me he's unusually sensitive to pain. He looked good to go upstairs even then."

"Doc, his oxygen saturation has decreased from ninety-seven percent to ninety-two percent in the last fifteen minutes. His respiratory rate has increased from twelve to thirty over that same period. He says he's feeling fine, but I'm getting uncomfortable. Can you take a look?"

The oxygen saturation (O_2 sat) was the percentage of oxygen-carrying capacity of its red blood cells the body actually utilized. Oxygen could be distributed to the body only when carried by red blood cells. The transfer of oxygen from the environment to the red blood cells occurred in the lungs. A decrease in the O_2 sat indicated the occurrence of one of only two possible causes. The first possible cause was a low oxygen concentration in the environment. In such a case there was insufficient oxygen for the lungs to deliver. This would happen, for example, if a person were locked in an impenetrable box and exhausted the oxygen within.

This definitely was not the case for Stan's patient lying in the recovery room. He must be suffering from the second possible cause: something had happened to his lungs, making them less capable of delivering oxygen to the red blood cells. Certainly a person could live with an O_2 sat much lower than 92 percent, and many cigarette smokers did. But any sudden change in lung function was ominous.

Stan's patient had more than doubled his respiratory rate in an unsuccessful effort to correct his decreasing ability to transfer oxygen from his lungs to his red blood cells, a situation demanding an explanation. Right now.

The patient in question, a twenty-eight-year-old white male, had shown up in the emergency room two days earlier, vomiting blood. The trip to the ER had followed a rousing, alcohol-fueled birthday bash the night prior to admission. His condition merited immediate admission and the transfusion of five units of blood. The bleeding hadn't stopped. And so, three hours ago, the patient entered the OR for surgery.

Jack had performed anesthesia for this patient in the usual manner. He'd drawn a blood sample immediately after induction of general anesthesia. This showed a blood count about half normal, thus demonstrating the need for further transfusion. Jack therefore gave him another three units of blood during the hour-and-twenty-minute operation. A general surgeon, Dr. Larry Walker, explored the abdomen and repaired and cauterized a bleeding area in the stomach. Everything went well, routinely well. The patient reached the recovery room at 7:35 p.m. A repeat blood count demonstrated improvement into the low-normal range. The patient awakened rapidly. He looked good; in fact, he looked much better than he had preop.

Jack had strolled into the recovery room at 8:00 p.m. to assess his patient's progress. "Hey, Bob, you look pretty good for someone who's just had an operation. How're you feeling?"

"Doc, I just need a little bit more of that morphine. You know, I'm more sensitive to pain than the average person. My family doctor told me so. Just don't go leaving the hospital until you make sure the nurses have enough pain medicine for me."

Jack was thus convinced Bob was out of danger. He'd asked the charge nurse to bring the evening's next customer to the operating room.

Jack had also told the charge nurse that he'd work in OR3 the rest of the evening. OR3 lay just across the hall from the recovery room. Jack preferred this arrangement—it ensured he remained readily available should some unexpected event endanger his previous patient. Postoperative complications requiring immediate intervention were rare. However, should such an event occur, the potential for disastrous consequence was real.

Stan leaned on the doorframe leading into OR3, keeping the door open. Jack said, "Could you open the door into the recovery room so I can see him?"

Stan walked across the hall, opened the door into the recovery room, and pushed the doorjamb into place. Jack's patient was twenty feet away, lying on a transport cart. His head was elevated thirty degrees above horizontal, and a green oxygen mask covered his face from the eyes down. A standard vital signs monitor hung from the ceiling directly over his head. The electrocardiogram (EKG) tracing demonstrated a normal contour, but the heart rate was 126—higher than Jack expected. The blood pressure was ninety over forty-six—fairly low for such a young man. The O_2 sat was 90 percent. Jack focused on the oxygen mask. He could see a cloud of water vapor appear on the mask with each exhalation and then disappear with each inhalation. The appearances and disappearances of the vapor cloud were happening much too rapidly.

The most sensitive part of the body to oxygen deprivation is the brain. Jack needed to check mental status in the most direct way. He shouted, "Hey, Bob, how're you doing? You feeling all right?"

Bob looked up to the sound of Jack's voice. "Doc, I'd feel better if you'd give me a little more morphine. My belly hurts."

Bob was getting at least an adequate supply of oxygen to his brain; after all, he could still complain. But his inhalations were not smooth. His chest displayed a rocking motion as his diaphragm struggled to get enough air into his lungs. Bob's neck muscles strained as they attempted to aid the diaphragm do its job. These signs, added to the undeniable fact that the O_2 sat was falling, presaged disaster.

Thoughts crashed into Jack's consciousness. *Was this guy having a heart attack? Had he just thrown a blood clot to his lungs? Why were his lungs failing? What's going on?*

"Bob, are you having any chest pain?"

"Doc, the only thing that hurts is my belly."

Jack spoke in a voice a little too loud. "Stan, draw arterial blood gases now. We can't figure out what's wrong with the lungs until we know the oxygen and carbon dioxide values. Then get an EKG. Better order a portable chest x-ray too. All of that STAT. And crank the oxygen all the way up."

Stan was already walking to the nurses' station for requisition slips. "Doc, the oxygen is all the way up. I'll make everything else happen right now."

"And, Stan, leave the door open so I can see him. Call Dr. Adams. He's on backup call for anesthesia."

A second recovery room nurse, Wendy Hill, had just discharged her only patient. She stood at Bob's side while Stan notified the lab of the emergent nature of the tests just ordered. Then Stan called Dr. Adams at home. Within a couple of minutes the appropriate people were on their way to the recovery room.

Stan walked back to the bedside and spoke to the patient. "Bob, we have to draw a little blood from the artery in your wrist. This may hurt a little."

Most patients used more graphic terms than "hurting just a little" to describe the insertion of a needle through the muscular wall of an artery. Stan cocked Bob's wrist back and gripped his hand and forearm firmly. Wendy felt carefully for the pulse then inserted a needle into the lumen of the radial artery. Bob yelled, "Fuck, what are you doing?" The pressure in the artery pushed the plunger of the syringe upward, confirming that the needle was indeed in an artery. What was remarkable to the two nurses—and even to Jack, standing twenty feet away—was the color of the blood. Arterial blood should be bright red. This blood was dark and had an almost bluish tinge.

Wendy capped the syringe and placed it in an ice-filled ziplock bag. Bob's O_2 sat dropped to 89 percent. His respiratory rate increased to forty. Wendy couldn't wait for an orderly to pick up the sample. She ran the arterial blood directly to the lab.

Jack watched this previously healthy young man deteriorate before his eyes. He knew he must make a life-or-death decision with incomplete data. For the patient, and for his physician, it had come to all or nothing.

Jack turned back to his patient on the operating room table. He'd continued to listen to the monitors in OR3 while observing the activity in the recovery room. If anything had sounded out of the ordinary, his attention would have immediately changed focus to determine the source of the auditory warning. Jack called the circulating nurse, Jerry Allison, to come and stand next to him.

"Jerry," he said in a quiet voice, "there's an immediate emergency with the last patient. I have to go to him. I want you to focus on this patient's vital signs on the monitor mounted on the top of the anesthesia machine. I'll be right across the hall. You'll be able to see me and talk to me. If anything changes, and I mean anything, I want you to sing out."

Jack turned to Dr. Kelly. "David, I have to go to the recovery room. I'm going to have Jerry stand here and watch your patient. Everything's stable. I've given your patient plenty of muscle relaxant so he won't move. Jerry will call me if anything changes."

The neurosurgeon was aware of unusual conversation in the doorway of OR3. He looked hard at Jack, a man with whom he'd worked for ten years. Their trust had been forged in the unforgiving environment of the operating room. Dr. Kelly said, "OK, Jack." His head dropped and he focused on the incision. "Sally, let's get this bone flap completed. Elevator, please."

Jack hurried across the hallway into the recovery room. Stan was at the patient's bedside and Wendy was entering the recovery room through the back door, returning from her trip to the lab. The patient was worse, his breathing shallow and labored. He looked up at Jack with the expression of a frightened child. Jack spoke to the nurses without taking his eyes off his patient. "We're out of time. Bring the intubation tray and crash cart to his bedside. Call respiratory therapy and tell them to bring a ventilator. After we place the breathing tube and get him on the ventilator, we'll place an arterial line and then a central line. Call x-ray and remind them we need a portable chest film right now."

Stan brought the necessary equipment on the run. Wendy moved to the nurses' station and made phone calls with urgency in her voice. Jack leaned over his patient. "Bob, I'm going to put you back to sleep and place a breathing tube into your trachea. Then I'm going to hook you up to a ventilator. I'll try to sedate you, but you may wake up and feel very weak. Don't let that scare you. Everyone here is caring for you."

Bob gasped. "I don't want any of that. I just need a little more morphine to feel better."

Jack looked into Bob's eyes. "I'm sorry. I don't have any more time to talk."

CHAPTER TWO

N ow beyond the explanation stage, Jack issued orders. "Stan, get a syringe of propofol and one of succinylcholine."

Stan located and checked the drugs. While he did that, Jack took a laryngoscope and an 8.5 millimeter endotracheal tube from the intubation tray, then turned to a drawer directly under the overhead vital signs monitor and pulled out a self-inflating bag and mask. He hooked a tube leading from the bag to an oxygen outlet and turned the flow of oxygen all the way up to fifteen liters. Jack looked at Stan to ensure he had attached the syringes to the patient's IV line. "Stan, give the propofol, then the succinylcholine."

The propofol induced unconsciousness within ten seconds. The muscle relaxant succinylcholine caused paralysis of all the patient's musculature five seconds later. Jack gave the patient several deep breaths of 100 percent oxygen with the breathing bag. The patient's chest moved up and down easily. His paralyzed muscles could not resist. Jack removed the mask from the patient's face, and the jaw fell loosely forward. He placed the laryngoscope into the mouth and swept the tongue to the left. The vocal cords were easy to see, white, with a space between them. Jack could even see into the trachea. He placed the endotracheal, or breathing, tube between the cords, watching it all the way. Then Jack extracted the laryngoscope from the patient's mouth and laid it on the pillow next to the patient's head. He attached the breathing bag to the endotracheal tube and squeezed. The lungs expanded, demonstrating Jack's control of the airway. Twenty-one seconds had elapsed since administration of the drugs

Jack continued breathing for the patient. He heard commotion as two respiratory therapists rushed through the recovery room's back door, pushing a ventilator to the bedside. One therapist attached the ventilator to the wall oxygen outlet with a hose. The other positioned himself at the head of the bed and took over hand ventilation of the patient. "What settings do you want, Doc?" he asked.

Jack gave orders in a distracted voice. "He'll need a breathing volume of one liter. Ten times a minute. Keep it at one hundred percent oxygen, and listen to his lungs periodically. Make sure both lungs keep expanding."

The patient's O_2 sat rebounded to 95 percent. Jack had been in the recovery room for eleven minutes. He walked back to the doorway of OR3. Nothing there had changed. Jack stood in the open doorway so he could observe both patients for whom he had responsibility. He looked at the clock in the OR. It'd been twenty minutes since his backup anesthesiologist, Dr. Ken Adams, had been called in from home. Dr. Adams, a dependable guy, would show up soon.

The phone at the recovery room nurses' station rang loudly. Wendy hurried to the desk, picked up, and identified herself. Jack heard her say, "Yes, we have that patient here." She listened intently, took a pen from her uniform pocket, and began writing numbers on a notepad. "Thank you." Wendy walked to Jack with the air of someone delivering bad news. She wordlessly handed the paper to Jack.

Jack looked at the paper. It confirmed what he'd observed clinically. The patient's oxygen content was half what it should be. His carbon dioxide was one-and-a-half times normal. The patient's lungs could not effectively transfer oxygen to his red blood cells, nor could they remove the product of respiration, carbon dioxide, from the blood. The patient was spinning downward, and the spiral was getting tighter.

The patient's rebound in O_2 sat occurred only because he was now mechanically ventilated. If Jack had waited for the lab results, if he'd waited for anything at all, his patient might well have deteriorated to the point where resuscitation would be difficult—or impossible. Jack didn't know what was causing the problem. He had to stabilize his patient and buy time until a diagnosis could be made.

Jack looked up from the lab sheet. "Wendy, call Dr. Walker. Tell him his patient is in critical condition. Then find out who's on call for internal medicine. He or she's got to come here now. Find out what's holding up x-ray and EKG. And get everything together for the arterial line."

"Yes, Doctor," Wendy said with unusual formality.

Jack walked into OR3. He confirmed with Jerry Allison that there'd been no change in the craniotomy patient's vital signs. He questioned Jerry about the specifics and progress of the case.

Jack pivoted back toward the recovery room when he heard the sounds of someone sprinting across the hallway. "Doc!" Stan shouted, "Come back to recovery room! His pressure is sixty!"

As Jack turned toward the recovery room, he spoke to the nurse he was leaving in OR3. "Jerry, stay where you are and keep doing what you're doing."

Jack focused on the vital signs monitor hanging above the recovery room patient. The pulse rate was now 140. The blood pressure 62. The O_2 sat 85 percent. "Wendy, open the crash cart. One cc of epinephrine, now." The blood pressure climbed to seventy-seven. "One more cc epinephrine." The next blood pressure climbed to one hundred fifteen. "Wendy, give this patient some Valium. It'll cause amnesia. He won't want to remember his resuscitation."

Jack looked to Stan. "I can feel a strong pulse. We need to place the arterial line now while his blood pressure is high." Stan reached into the crash cart and handed Jack a catheter. Then he pulled the now unresisting patient's forearm out with the wrist extended backward. Jack repeated the procedure Wendy had used to draw the initial blood gas sample, except this time he inserted a small catheter into the radial artery. He pulled the needle from within the catheter's lumen. Blood pulsed out of the catheter, confirming its proper placement inside the patient's radial artery. Jack attached a length of tubing Wendy offered him to the catheter. The tubing in turn was connected to a pressure transducer. This device translated the pulsing pressure inside the artery into a waveform on the vital signs monitor. It also generated a numerical readout of the blood pressure generated by each beat of the heart.

The arterial line enabled the patient's doctors and nurses to titrate the potent drugs necessary for resuscitation on a very exact basis. It also allowed the checking of laboratory specimens frequently. These tools would help the care providers keep this patient alive just a little longer.

Jack believed these measures would enable him to seize control of the situation. He intended to keep this man alive until a diagnosis could be made and definitive therapy instituted. He was still the methodical professional who'd not allow himself the luxury of negative thinking. He'd been in tough situations many times in the past. His instincts and knowledge, and what he believed to be his good luck, had allowed him to escape disaster every time. Dr. Jack Andrews would come through again.

The patient's blood pressure began a steady drift to ninety-two. Jack spoke quietly. "Wendy, he can't maintain blood pressure unless we support him with drugs. Give him one cc of epinephrine every time his pressure goes below eighty. Stan, call pharmacy and have them set up an epinephrine drip. We'll drip it in slowly and try to smooth out this roller coaster ride of high and low pressures."

Stan and Wendy maintained the blood pressure with small doses of epinephrine over the next twelve minutes until the epinephrine drip arrived. Jack spoke to his nurses while staring at the monitor. "Titrate that drug in. Keep his pressure between ninety and a hundred thirty."

The back door to the recovery room swung open. An EKG technician entered, pushing her small, light machine ahead of her. Behind her came two x-ray techs, awkwardly manhandling their much larger machine. Jack spoke to the entire room. "Get me the chest x-ray first. Don't wait for the radiologist to read it. Bring it right back to me. Then get the EKG. Stan, call Dr. Walker again. Tell him his patient is extremely critical, and if he wants to have any input, he'd better get here. Did you find who's on call for internal medicine?"

Stan replied, "Dr. Kim Stevens is on call. She's at the other hospital, but says she'll be here ASAP."

"All right, Stan. Page her again and tell her this is serious. Then draw another blood gas sample. Get it from the arterial line. And find out where Dr. Adams is—he's got to take over the craniotomy."

Jack crossed the hallway to check on his other patient. He just cleared the doorway when he heard Stan running in behind him. "Doc, his pressure is forty."

Jack would never remember leaving OR3. Suddenly, he was in the recovery room at Bob's bedside. "Wendy, give him a bolus of epinephrine now."

Jack looked up as the back door to the recovery room opened. Dr. Ken Adams walked in. Jack spoke quietly, consciously modulating his voice. "Ken, I've got a real problem here. There's a craniotomy across the hall. He was healthy until he got a bump on his head. You've got to take over his anesthesia."

Dr. Ken Adams took in all the activity in the recovery room. The ventilator, the portable x-ray machine, the EKG tech. He noticed the vital signs monitor demonstrated an arterial line tracing. Dr. Adams, an experienced anesthesiologist, was instantly glad he had no responsibility for what was occurring in the recovery room. Without saying a word he headed across the hall to OR3.

The patient responded to the epinephrine bolus, his blood pressure rose to 106. "Stan, double the dose of the epinephrine drip. From now on, don't wait for the blood pressure to sag. Crank the epi up immediately in response to any decrease in blood pressure. Wendy, we have to place a central line. If he's bleeding somewhere, his central pressure will be low. If his heart is failing and can't push blood forward through the aorta, his central pressure will be high. I have to know which is the case."

Wendy moved a platform just to the left of the patient's head. On it, she placed a sterile kit for placement of a line to measure central venous pressure (CVP). Then she tilted the bed so the head was lower than the feet. Placing the head lower than the feet caused the jugular vein to distend, giving Jack a larger target. Jack turned the head forty-five degrees to the left and painted the neck with iodine solution. He pulled on a sterile gown and gloves, then lifted drapes from the kit and isolated the painted, sterile area. Jack felt the neck and determined where the major neck muscles formed an inverted V just outside the carotid artery. The carotid, the main artery to the brain, must be avoided. He infiltrated local anesthetic into the skin just over his target area. This ensured that the patient, who was sedated but not fully asleep, would not react to the needle stick. Jack placed a large bore needle into the center of the anesthetized area and aimed to the patient's right side. The needle advanced less than an inch when it entered the internal jugular vein. Jack pulled dark-red blood through the needle into the syringe. The color relieved him. Had he been off course, bright red blood would have indicated he'd struck the carotid artery.

Jack took the syringe off the hub of the needle and placed the index finger of his left hand over the end of the needle to keep blood from flowing out. With his right hand, he pulled a thin wire out of the kit and passed it through the lumen of the needle and straight down into the internal jugular vein. The wire passed with little resistance. The EKG monitor registered a missed beat. This told Jack the wire had entered the heart and stimulated it. The wire was indeed central.

"Good," Jack said to Wendy, "it's in the right place." He backed the wire out slightly to prevent any further missed beats. Jack withdrew the needle over the wire, leaving only the wire in the vein. He took a catheter from the kit and threaded it over the wire into place, with the catheter's distal end just above the heart. Then he withdrew the wire, while holding the catheter motionless. Finally, he connected the catheter to a transducer identical to the one monitoring arterial blood pressure.

"OK, Stan, return the bed to level. This guy's got enough problems breathing, we don't want to make things worse by keeping his head down."

The central venous pressure, now displayed on the vital signs monitor right under the arterial blood pressure, was six. This was low— in fact, half of normal. The patient's blood volume was low despite the fact there was no sign of bleeding. Jack increased the volume of fluid administered to the patient. He expected the CVP to rise. But it remained unchanged. Even more impressive was the absolute correlation of blood pressure with epinephrine dose. A precipitous drop in arterial blood pressure immediately followed even a slight decrease in the rate of epinephrine administration.

He turned to his recovery room nurses. "It's got to be an allergic reaction, but I don't know to what. I looked at his medical record before his operation. He never had any medical allergies before, and he showed no reaction to anything we gave him during his operation. He was steady as a rock."

"Could he be reacting to something else?" Stan asked. "Maybe it's not a reaction to a drug."

"Could be. Maybe he developed an allergy to the latex in the surgical field. Maybe there was something in one of those units of blood. Our only hope is to keep him alive and hope he rides out the reaction."

The x-ray and EKG technicians were still standing at the entryway of the recovery room in rapt attention. "OK," Jack said, "come on. Get the portable chest x-ray first."

The two x-ray techs rolled the portable machine to the bedside. Stan and Wendy helped one of them lean the patient forward at the waist while the second tech placed an x-ray cassette behind him. They laid the patient down gently on the hard cassette, murmuring apologies. The two techs put on lead aprons and yelled, "X-ray." Stan and Wendy hurriedly moved ten feet from the bedside. Jack, unconcerned, didn't move away from his patient. The machine emitted a burring noise and took the x-ray. One of the techs eased the cassette out from behind the patient and ran to get the film developed. The second tech moved the machine away from the bedside, where it, and she, would remain until the quality of the first film had been assured.

Next, the EKG tech attached the necessary twelve leads to the patient. The machine demonstrated a normal EKG, except the heart was beating unusually fast. There were no signs of a heart attack. Whatever else was going wrong, the heart was performing well.

Suddenly, everyone heard the sound of someone running. The x-ray tech ran in, x-ray in hand. He slid to a halt in front of the viewing box, and, without a word, attached the film. Jack stared at the film, transfixed. Both lungs appeared almost completely white—they were full of fluid. A physician would characterize the finding as pulmonary edema. A layperson could accurately surmise the patient was drowning.

Stan was first to speak, his voice sounding far away. "How can he still be alive? And how can he have an O_2 sat in the nineties?"

Fighting despair, Jack said, "The ventilator's keeping him alive. It's blowing the lungs up like balloons. The positive pressure the ventilator is generating is forcing oxygen into the lungs. That same pressure is pushing against blood vessels, making it harder for them to leak more fluid into the lung tissue. Without that pressure this guy would already be dead."

The ventilator was buying just a little more time for this patient to stay alive.

Jack sounded as if he were talking to himself. "We've got to get rid of the fluid. Got to mobilize it from the lung tissue and get it back into blood vessels so it can be delivered to the kidneys. Then he can pee it out. How much urine is he making?"

Wendy looked down at the patient's urine bag. "Doctor, he made thirty cc his first forty-five minutes in the recovery room, but he's made only five cc since."

"If we don't get the fluid out of his lungs he's a dead man. We have to give him a diuretic. We'll try Lasix and hope it gets his kidneys working."

Stan spoke up. "But Doc, if you get him making a lot of urine, won't that drop the volume of fluid in his blood vessels? We can't keep his blood pressure up now—how are we going to keep it up if there's less blood?"

"What you're saying is right," Jack replied softly. "If we get him peeing enough to get rid of the lung fluid, his blood pressure will drop. But if we don't succeed in getting rid of the fluid, he'll die. We have to hope he can live with lower blood pressure. He's young and that might give him an edge. We'll increase the epinephrine dose to maintain pressure as best we can."

Wendy, who had studied pharmacology in nursing school, observed, "But isn't it true that high dose epinephrine makes the kidneys less efficient?"

Jack said, "That's true, and bad for us and bad for the patient. But I'm out of options. Give him twenty milligrams of Lasix intravenously now."

Jack walked over to the x-ray screen to look for some hope in the film just taken. He spun around as Stan shouted, "Shit, Doc, look at this."

Fluid was coming out of the endotracheal tube. It had the amber color of light beer. There was a lot of it. It flowed down through the hose connecting the endotracheal tube to the ventilator. It settled in the dependent portions of the hose and was rapidly working its way back, closer and closer to the patient.

Fluid was moving out of the lungs' blood vessels and into the spaces where oxygen exchange normally occurred. There was so much fluid escaping the blood vessels that the fluid was being forced out of the lungs and right out through the endotracheal tube. It was as if a faucet were dripping fluid out of the lungs.

Jack sounded hopeless, "The vascular integrity has completely broken down. The vessels can't hold fluid anymore. The fluid is yellow because the holes in the vessels are large enough to allow fluid and protein to escape, but they aren't large enough to let the red blood cells through—yet. We have to get the fluid out or he'll drown."

Everyone knew what was necessary. With unspoken precision the drill began. Stan and Wendy pulled on clean gloves. Stan attached a long, large bore catheter to a length of suction hose. Wendy disconnected the endotracheal tube from the ventilator and turned the ventilator off. Stan pushed the catheter through the lumen of the endotracheal tube and suctioned out fluid. This caused a loud slurping sound. Stan removed the catheter. Wendy hooked the breathing bag to the endotracheal tube and gave the patient six large breaths of 100 percent oxygen. Then she disconnected the breathing bag and Stan reinserted the catheter to remove more of the amber fluid. They repeated this procedure continuously, never stopping to rest. Stan and Wendy never gave up. They kept the patient alive.

CHAPTER THREE

Jack stepped away from the bed five minutes after Stan and Wendy began their life-preserving efforts. What he saw astounded him. The patient was swelling everywhere.

For a physician, edema is fluid that is somewhere it shouldn't be, but the term was too mild to describe what Jack saw.

Jack pushed a finger against his patient's upper arm. When he pulled his finger away, an indentation remained. It was half an inch deep. "No, no, no." Jack couldn't hide his emotions. "This guy is edematous everywhere. Everything is swelling. His face, his arms, his torso, his legs. Look at his eyes."

Bob's eyes looked as if they were in a deep hole.

"He's not just leaking fluid into his lungs. He's leaking everywhere. That's why we can't keep his blood pressure up. That's why his kidneys aren't working. All the fluid we've given him is just going into his tissues. None of it is staying in his blood vessels. The reason we saw it in the lungs first was because fluid in the lungs is visible on a chest x-ray. Everywhere else it goes into tissue and accumulates. We didn't notice it because we had to focus on his lungs just to keep him alive minute to minute. But the loss of vascular integrity is not just in the lungs—it's everywhere in his body."

Jack looked up as Dr. Kim Stevens, the internal medicine physician on call for the night, strolled into the recovery room. Dr. Stevens believed Dr. Andrews had called her because of a simple case of pulmonary edema in a postop patient. She was annoyed because she'd been paged several times.

On her way across town from the other hospital she'd reflected on what she, as an internist, perceived to be a common problem in the operating room. Some careless, or clueless, anesthesiologist had overloaded a patient with too much IV fluid. Then the patient's O$_2$ sat had decreased. And to think that same anesthesiologist made more money than an intellectual, gifted physician like herself. She planned to give the patient a cursory examination then administer a stiff dose of Lasix. The Lasix would start a brisk flow of urine that would, in turn, clear the fluid from his lungs. The lungs would improve immediately, and Dr. Stevens would continue supplemental oxygen overnight. Tomorrow morning a chest x-ray would demonstrate marked improvement. The steps in therapy were routine. Stevens would bill for her management of an intensive care patient. Not as much as she deserved, and not as much as that anesthesiologist had collected, but a nice fee nonetheless. She sure hoped this patient had good insurance.

As Stevens approached Jack she made no effort to hide her disdain for operating room physicians. They were nothing but intellectually inferior plumbers. It was time to save the cowboys again.

The fact this case was not routine became apparent to her only when she reached the bedside. A female nurse was breathing for the patient. A male nurse, also at the head of the bed, was holding a large suction catheter. Mounted on the wall behind the patient were four large canisters. Three were full of yellow fluid. Jack Andrews, the anesthesiologist, stood at the foot of the bed. He looked exhausted.

The first thought entering Stevens's mind was, *What has this guy screwed up?* She didn't say that. Instead she asked, "What's going on? This patient looks sick."

Jack knew exactly what she was thinking. Jack regarded internists like Kim Stevens as know-it-all pricks who gave all sorts of advice about why a problem had occurred, but were incapable of actually doing anything themselves when a patient was critically endangered. Jack, however, needed another perspective. It never hurt to get an internist's opinion on the chart, especially when that internist was forced to deal in the here and now. At this moment, and just like Jack, Stevens possessed less than complete data. She nonetheless was expected to successfully treat this patient.

Jack replied in his most professional manner, "The patient had an eighty-minute procedure for a stomach bleed that finished at seven thirty-five this evening. During the operation he received three units of blood and fifteen hundred cc of normal saline. He woke up uneventfully. About forty-five minutes after reaching the recovery room his O_2 sat dropped, although never below eighty-five percent. He was reintubated and placed on a ventilator. His O_2 sat is now ninety-six percent. He's requiring epinephrine to keep his blood pressure at acceptable levels. His chest x-ray demonstrates severe pulmonary edema. He's not made urine since the episode began. We've just given him twenty milligrams of Lasix, but it's had no effect. His central pressure is low so he isn't overloaded with fluid in the usual sense. Fluid accumulating in the lungs has begun flowing out of his endotracheal tube and the quantity is huge. Something has compromised the integrity of his entire vascular system. He's leaking everywhere. I think it's some kind of allergic reaction. Maybe a reaction to the blood transfusion. Maybe it's to one of the drugs he received. I just don't know. We have to support him until a diagnosis can be made."

Stevens did not understand the cause of this event, but she was sure someone of her intellectual ability could sort things out. Probably this anesthesiologist, really just an overpaid technician, had somehow overloaded the patient with fluid and had caused pulmonary edema. The patient's low central pressure troubled her a little, but perhaps this young patient normally ran low central pressures. Now was the time for Kim Stevens to demonstrate how a real doctor dealt with a serious problem.

She began speaking as she stared at the vital signs monitor, her back to Jack. She spoke at the nurses, not to them, and ignored Jack completely. "We have to stop this process. We'll begin by giving him large doses of steroids and Benadryl to counter any possible allergic reaction. Obviously he'll require much larger doses of Lasix. After we get some of this fluid off-loaded we'll get him off the ventilator. Then we can begin to wean the epinephrine."

Jack knew he had to let Kim Stevens try things her own way. He thought it entirely likely this patient was heading toward a bad outcome. It was best to demonstrate another physician's methods had undergone an honest trial. His own management had kept the patient alive, but only barely. Jack hadn't come up with a diagnosis or a comprehensive plan for therapy.

Jack replied, "I certainly hope those maneuvers help. I advise you to be cautious. We've not been able to maintain blood pressure without epinephrine."

At 10:15 P.M. Dr. Larry Walker called from his car. He was en route to the hospital. Jack updated him on his patient's condition.

Walker became agitated. "Hey, this guy was OK during the operation. Whatever happened to him must have happened in the recovery room. What did you do? Let him aspirate? This is not because of anything I did. Put Stevens on the phone."

Kim Stevens took the phone and listened for a moment. "Larry, everything will be all right. I can handle this. Just come in and talk to the family. I'll initiate therapy and take the patient to the intensive care unit. See you in a few minutes."

Jack understood. When there's a bad result in the operating room, it's imperative to affix blame…on someone else. Few physicians, and even fewer lawyers, will acknowledge that, on occasion, a patient can experience a bad outcome even though no one did anything wrong. It is more expedient, and safer, to identify a culprit and condemn him with a few well-chosen words.

Jack sat at the nurses' station and watched. He was no longer in charge. The surgeon, the patient's primary physician, had designated another physician to care for his patient.

During his pauses in suctioning, while Wendy breathed for the patient, Stan carried out the orders Dr. Stevens issued in rapid succession. The epinephrine was gradually turned down. One hundred milligrams of Lasix was injected intravenously. The blood pressure sagged. The patient made no urine. Wendy continued to breathe for the patient and Stan continued to suction. One canister after another filled with amber fluid. The central pressure drifted down to half its former value. Dr. Stevens refused to increase the rate of IV fluid administration because she feared overloading the patient.

The patient's entire body continued to swell. His head grew as if it were a balloon being inflated.

Every possible complication of every intervention occurred. The patient had few of his own physiological defenses remaining.

Dr. Larry Walker strode into the recovery room. He looked frightened—no, Jack decided—he looked angry. He managed, with effort, to look at Jack and nod as he walked past the nurses' station, his face a mask. He walked straight to the foot of the bed and spoke to Dr. Stevens with theatrical loudness. "I don't understand what's happening here. This patient had no problems in the operating room. What happened here in the recovery room?"

Dr. Stevens replied sanctimoniously, "Well, I think he's in congestive heart failure. Most likely overloaded. I'll fix it."

Jack ruefully mused that Dr. Stevens had somehow forgotten about the amber fluid cascading out of the patient's lungs. Or maybe she'd chosen to ignore that bit of information because it didn't fit into any easily treated diagnosis.

Suddenly, the blood pressure dropped to fifty-five. Stevens and Walker both registered surprise. Then Stevens yelled, "Double that epinephrine drip now!"

Jack was already on his feet, running to the bedside.

The blood pressure climbed back into the eighties within sixty seconds.

Jack confronted the two physicians in front of him. "The patient is not getting better despite your intervention. In fact, he's going to die because we can't oxygenate him and we can't keep his blood pressure anywhere near normal. There's only one chance. We have to put him on cardiopulmonary bypass as if he were having open-heart surgery. If we support him totally maybe this reaction will run its course. That's the only chance we have of keeping him alive. We should call the heart surgery team immediately."

Stevens and Walker were dumbfounded, then overtly hostile. To attempt such radical therapy was an admission something had gone very wrong, something they were incapable of controlling. It was an admission of defeat, or possibly of fault. Walker spoke first. "This is my patient. He's not going to undergo cardiopulmonary bypass to treat some reaction that followed a routine belly case. This wild idea of yours is dangerous and unnecessary."

Dr. Stevens was slowly and emphatically shaking her head. She spoke to Jack as if she were a teacher instructing a mediocre student. "We'll rid this patient of pulmonary edema with the standard methods. I'll determine all the variables. We'll find a way to support his blood pressure and get him in proper fluid balance. Need I remind you, Dr. Andrews, that the risks from cardiopulmonary bypass are not negligible? You look tired. Perhaps you should go somewhere and rest."

Jack began walking away from the patient, then turned and said, "You don't get it. All the usual therapy has failed. He won't live unless something radical is attempted. I'll be around when you finally reach the only decision that'll give him a chance." Jack sat down at the nurses' station.

Drs. Stevens and Walker turned their backs to Jack and faced the patient. It was time to get down to business and ignore this anesthesia technician. Jack disagreed with them and lacked confidence in their abilities. That lack of confidence of and by itself demonstrated he was incapable of good judgment.

Over the next hour the two physicians issued constant orders, but nothing helped. The patient required more and more epinephrine. He became grotesquely swollen. His blood pressure slipped into the seventies. Then it passed through the sixties. Death was near.

Jack's frustration mounted. He angrily approached the bedside and looked directly at his detractors. Kim Stevens was shell-shocked, close to tears. She found it impossible to conceive she couldn't find the answer. But Larry Walker was still the picture of the carefully groomed surgeon in the expensive suit, not a hair out of place. He maintained the air of a savior come to solve problems caused by someone else.

Jack spoke through clenched teeth. "We have to call the heart team. Otherwise, we have a dead man."

22

Walker replied as if he were talking to a frightened patient prior to a dangerous operation. He was, after all, someone who didn't suffer from the human condition of making personal mistakes. "OK, get them in. But remember, this is on your head. The patient was fine at the end of the operation. Whatever caused this disaster happened in the recovery room. You make the arrangements. I'll talk to the family."

Jack hurried to the phone. As he dialed he considered how difficult it would be for Larry Walker to find the family. The patient's drinking buddies had dropped him off at the hospital two days earlier. They hadn't returned.

Jack first called the hospital charge nurse and asked her to phone the four nurses necessary for a heart operation. It would take them several minutes to set up the operating room, so those nurses had to be contacted first. Then he called the cardiopulmonary perfusionist, Glenn Mason. The machine that enabled physicians to fully support the patient during cardiopulmonary bypass must be assembled, a job requiring maybe ten minutes. Glenn sleepily picked up his bedside phone on the second ring. He was on his way to the hospital in five minutes.

Jack then phoned the cardiac surgeon. Dr. Harry Herbert was an unusual heart surgeon. In a profession of prima donnas he stood out as an individual who required no posturing to convince his coworkers of his talent. He led his team by example, and his team worked hard to come up to his level. Jack was one of four anesthesiologists with whom Dr. Herbert worked regularly. Jack considered it a privilege to be trusted by this man.

The phone rang. "This is Herbert."

"Hello, Harry. This is Jack Andrews. I have a real problem. We did an operation earlier this evening for a stomach bleed and now the patient has developed some kind of reaction I can't explain. He's leaking fluid everywhere. We have to suction his lungs every six breaths to maintain minimal acceptable O_2 sats. His entire body is grossly edematous. There's no urine output. His blood pressure is extremely low despite maximum epinephrine therapy. I'd like to support him on cardiopulmonary bypass and hope this will eventually blow over. Otherwise, this guy is going to die very soon. I see no other way."

Harry Herbert instinctively recoiled as he listened to the clinical summary. He was being asked to get involved in another physician's problem. Even worse, the suggested therapy was radical, probably even untried. He was being asked to suspend his own judgment, and, on Jack Andrew's word, initiate therapy that had little, if any, support in the medical literature. Merely suggesting it indicated there'd almost certainly be a bad outcome. One way or another everyone involved was going to be asked questions by very unpleasant people, people with a financial stake in making sure this decision was made to look bad.

Herbert replied carefully, "Jack, what you're asking me to do is very difficult. I realize this is a preexisting problem, but how am I going to justify my actions? The reputation of the entire heart team is on the line."

"Harry, this man's going to die unless we try something extraordinary. I know what I'm asking you to do."

Harry Herbert thought hard about professional duty, about duty to a patient, and duty to his team. "All right, I'll take a look. What's the status of the heart team?"

"They're on the way. They'll be ready when you get here."

"I'll be there in fifteen minutes. Jack, find another way before I arrive."

Jack looked back to the patient. His blood pressure was in the forties, his heart rate 168. Dr. Stevens robotically dispensed orders to increase the epinephrine dose. She'd become a discouraged, noncontributing physician. The O_2 sat remained at 90 percent. This was a testament to Stan and Wendy's continued hand ventilation and suctioning of the patient, their refusal to quit.

The first of the cardiac surgery nurses arrived in the recovery room. She scanned the room and assumed Jack was in charge. Nikki Watkins took pride in her assertive manner. "What's the deal?" she demanded. "The charge nurse told me to get here ASAP, but didn't have a clue about what we're supposed to do. Fill me in."

Jack spoke to Nikki Watkins the way an army officer spoke to his most experienced chief master sergeant. "This patient is going to arrest in the next few minutes. We have to split his sternum and get him on bypass before that happens. All we need are the instruments necessary to begin an open-heart case. As soon as all the instruments are ready we're taking this guy to the operating room. We'll get the chest prepped and draped. When Dr. Herbert gets here, you're going to hand him a scalpel, then the sternal saw, and we're going to go on bypass. Any questions?"

"Bring him back to the OR in five minutes. A couple of nurses will help you position and prep the patient while the circulating nurse and I get instruments ready. Glenn is already setting up the pump." Nikki left Jack and hurried down the hall.

Jack turned to Wendy. "I'll take over the breathing. Get a portable oxygen tank. Then get the transducers, the IV lines, and an epinephrine drip attached to one IV pole for the trip down the hall. We go in five minutes."

It took Wendy four minutes to prepare for the trip. Stan suctioned vigorously one last time. Jack connected the breathing bag to the portable oxygen tank. They began their exit from the recovery room. Wendy pushed the foot of the bed and steered as Jack pushed the bed with his left hand while bagging with his right. Stan followed with the IV pole. No one spoke to Drs. Stevens or Walker. The trip, sixty feet down the hallway to the cardiac surgery operating room, seemed to take an eternity.

When they reached the operating room two surgical nurses met them and replaced Stan and Wendy. As they pushed the bed into the OR Jack turned to the two exhausted recovery room nurses. They seemed stranded, unable to decide what to do or where to go. "You two have done everything that could be done. Thanks. Now go home. I'll let you know what happens."

The OR crew positioned the patient's bed against the operating room table. Nikki Watkins, already scrubbed, continued to set up the sterile operating instruments. The other three cardiac nurses, Glenn Mason, and Jack each picked up part of the sheet laying underneath the patient and, on the count of three, moved him to the operating table.

Glenn left the table to complete preparation of the cardiopulmonary bypass machine. Jack connected the endotracheal tube to the anesthesia machine, ensured the machine was delivering 100 percent oxygen, and turned the ventilator on. Two of the cardiac nurses assisted Nikki's preparation. The fourth nurse tucked the patient's arms against his sides with towels. Jack attached all the monitors to his anesthesia machine. The heart rate read 172; the blood pressure, forty-two; the central venous pressure, one; the O_2 sat, 90 percent.

Jack located the suction catheter on his anesthesia machine. He began the task of suctioning the lungs once every six breaths. Amber fluid flowed unabated.

The phone on the wall rang. The circulating nurse answered and then addressed the room. "That's Dr. Herbert. He's in the locker room changing into scrubs. He said we should prep the chest."

The patient arrested just as a nurse started to apply iodine solution to the surgical field.

The EKG changed from a rapid regular rhythm, one in which all the heartbeats appeared identical, to an irregular line moving in a random pattern. Simultaneously the arterial waveform went flat and recorded a pressure of zero. The heart was fibrillating. It was no longer a pump. It had become a twitching sack.

Jack yelled, "Get Dr. Herbert here now." He began pushing down on the sternum at a rate of one hundred per minute. Each compression caused a slight increase in blood pressure, an increase too weak to register as a digital readout on the vital signs monitor. There was very little blood being pumped to the brain or the heart or to any other organ. The patient was close to death.

Dr. Herbert appeared in the room. Jack hadn't seen him arrive. He shouted to his team, "We don't have time to split the chest. We'll go fem-fem. Throw some iodine over his groin. Just give me a gown and gloves. I don't have time to scrub. Is the pump ready?"

Glenn Mason pushed the pump close to the OR table. "I'm ready. We can cannulate."

Nikki handed Dr. Herbert sterile drapes to isolate the area already drenched with iodine. His right hand went up, and she placed a scalpel in it. He made a wide incision, encompassing the groin area. There was no pulse to use as a landmark, but, experience showing, Dr. Herbert found the femoral artery and its adjacent vein. He made an incision into the femoral artery, placed a cannula as large as his thumb into the artery, and sutured it into place so there were no leaks. He repeated the procedure on the femoral vein. As soon as the second cannula was secured Dr. Herbert turned to Glenn Mason. "On bypass."

The cardiopulmonary bypass machine whirred into action. Blood was extracted from the femoral vein, circulated through the machine where the red blood cells were oxygenated, and finally pumped into the femoral artery under pressure. The cardiopulmonary machine forced oxygenated blood through the body's vascular system. It replaced the patient's lungs and heart. It supported him a little longer.

Dr. Herbert looked up at Jack. "Could you shock this guy and see if his heart will start?"

Jack reached for the defibrillation paddles permanently housed under the bedside bank of monitors. He placed one paddle over the right side of the sternum and the other over the lateral side of the left chest. He charged the paddles and yelled, "Clear." Everyone moved away from the OR table and Jack discharged the paddles. The patient's body arched upward a few inches. The heart, now enriched by oxygenated blood supplied by the pump, immediately began to beat in a regular rhythm. It happened quickly, as if someone had just flipped an "on" switch.

Now the operating room team began the wait. They used the pump to respond to the patient's disorders. The huge cannulas could introduce liters of fluid into the patient in seconds. The pump could keep blood pressure up by increasing its flow. With the benefit of immediate feedback to their therapy, physicians in the cardiac room could immediately correct blood counts and electrolyte imbalances.

The team repeatedly corrected all these variables during the next five hours. All blood values were kept in normal range. The central pressure stayed within acceptable levels with the infusion of more fluid. But urine never flowed. The patient's inability to keep fluid in his vascular tree caused him to swell more and more. He no longer appeared real. He resembled a grotesquely swollen doll.

CHAPTER FOUR

After five hours, Harry Herbert spoke quietly, "Jack, there's nothing left to do. The reaction, whatever it is, isn't going to end. Everything leaks everywhere. It's time to quit."

Jack had been suctioning the endotracheal tube when Harry Herbert began speaking. He stopped suctioning. The amber fluid dripped out of the disconnected tube like water from a leaky faucet. Drip. Drip. Drip. An ever-expanding puddle formed on the floor. Jack looked at his friend. "You're right. We can't save this man. It's over."

Dr. Herbert looked at Glenn Mason. Glenn looked back; he wouldn't stop without an order. "Glenn, off bypass."

The cardiopulmonary bypass machine stopped and the patient's blood pressure immediately plummeted to zero. The EKG monitor demonstrated ventricular fibrillation for the second time. No one pushed on the chest. No one charged the paddles. After a few minutes the fibrillation pattern went completely flat. The patient was dead.

Harry spoke again to Jack. "Go somewhere and rest. We'll get him closed. Then you and I can speak to the family."

"There's no family here," Jack mumbled. "This guy was all alone."

"OK. When I'm done, I'll call the chaplain's office. They'll track down any family. Then I'll call the primary physician. It's Larry Walker, right? Jack, you look bad. You can't help anyone anymore. Go on and get out of here."

Jack walked down the hallway and back to the recovery room. It was 5:10 a.m. The room, illuminated only by a reading light at the nurses' station, was still. The day shift wouldn't arrive until 6:00 a.m.

Jack sat down on a rolling stool. He pushed back until the stool stopped against the wall. He stared into the darkness, uncertain of his feelings. He genuinely regretted the death of a young patient. He thought about his actions during the past several hours. If he'd done everything right, wouldn't the patient still be alive? He reminded himself not to think that way, not to condemn himself, especially when he was depressed and exhausted. But he knew he'd second-guess himself for a long time. There was going to be a lot of second-guessing. He knew he faced professional and legal problems. Lawyers were coming, and they'd be aided by his fellow physicians, ever anxious to avoid personal responsibility. Jack Andrews would inevitably become the fall guy.

The surest way for a doctor to avoid responsibility was to find someone else to blame. There was never outright condemnation of one physician by another. Instead, a physician would hint that something someone else had done was not quite right. *This is going to get ugly,* Jack thought hopelessly.

About half an hour after Jack reached the recovery room the overhead lights flicked on. Two operating room nurses wheeled the blanket-covered patient into the room on a transport cart. The nurses started when they realized Jack was sitting there. They remained quiet. One of them took the patient's chart, which was on top of the blanket, and carried it to the nurses' station. She placed it on the desk as far from Jack as she could get. Both nurses hurried away, never speaking. They flicked the lights out as they left.

Jack stared at the chart, then looked over to his patient, a person he'd talked to only a few hours earlier. How could this man be dead? Jack had never felt so tired. The darkness became more than the absence of light. It had a presence. Jack wanted to stay in the darkness.

The overhead lights came on again. Jack looked up to see Harry Herbert standing a few feet away. "Jack, there's nothing to be done. No one did anything wrong, especially you. You made sure your patient got his best shot. Don't get into one of those self-abusive doctor fits now."

Jack stood up. "Thanks, Harry. For coming and trying. For helping me."

"Jack, I'll make sure Larry Walker's made aware of what happened. I'll have the chaplain coordinate with him to find the family. You go home."

Jack began walking toward the locker room. He didn't look back. The hallway was barely illuminated. Jack wanted the darkness to envelop him.

CHAPTER FIVE

Jack went into the locker room and rapidly changed into street clothes. His post-call status guaranteed he had no hospital responsibilities today. He wanted to get out before the day shift arrived.

Jack didn't want to answer questions. He knew the staff would learn of the death in the OR within minutes of their arrival. They'd talk about how the end had come just before they'd reported to work and how relieved they were not to be involved. The departing nursing staff would anxiously impart their knowledge, incomplete and superficial as it was, to everyone they encountered. Some of the physicians, mostly the less talented ones, would express conjecture on what had happened or give sanctimonious statements of sympathy, none of which Jack wanted to hear. He walked out, head down.

He went straight to the physicians' parking lot, the one closest to the building. His green Land Rover, the perfect car for a successful physician, was parked in a spot reserved for on-call personnel. He pulled on a stylish pair of aviator sunglasses, started the engine, and began the fifteen-minute drive home.

Jack wanted to go home. He wanted to get away from the hospital. He didn't want to see his wife.

Jack first encountered his wife twelve very long years ago during his anesthesia residency. He'd been young and testosterone driven and had little time away from the demands of his training. Kate worked as an operating room nurse at university hospitals. She'd made a career decision to become a doctor's wife, a dream she pursued with energy and resourcefulness. On a few previous occasions she'd almost succeeded, but somehow never managed to close the deal. She was twenty-six years old and time was running out. Age disadvantage stared her in the face. Competition was fierce at university hospitals.

Kate became available for Jack. His life consisted of long hours in the operating room, occasional workouts when he wasn't completely exhausted, and an hour or two of study each evening in preparation for anesthesia boards. The rest of his time he spent with Kate. She prepared him nice meals, and then invariably led him straight to bed. Jack was dimly aware of Kate's very active past, but all could be forgiven. She made him feel good. In the insecure and sometimes frightening world of a young person learning to perform in the operating room where no mistake was tolerated, someone who made him feel good was of supreme value.

They married right after Jack completed his residency. Kate produced two children as quickly as possible. Then she suddenly discovered that sex was distasteful—at least it was with Jack. And she got everything she wanted. Jack tolerated almost anything to avoid her never-ending complaints. In moments of reflection, Jack marveled at the acting ability she displayed before their marriage.

Jack parked the Land Rover in the garage and walked into the house. His two children, ages ten and eight, were, as usual, getting their own breakfasts. Jennifer, the older of the two, shouted, "Sarah, hurry up with the carton of milk. I don't have all day to wait. All you ever do is ruin my life."

"Really?" Sarah yelled back. "Well, maybe you should find someone else to boss around." She pushed the milk across the table as slowly as possible.

To Jack's chagrin they were learning rapidly from their mother.

Shouting emanated from the master bedroom. "Do I have to listen to you two fight all the time?" *Remarkable*, thought Jack. Kate was actually awake before the kids got off to school.

Jennifer looked up at her father. "Oh, hi, Dad. Can you make Sarah hurry up? We have to meet the bus in fifteen minutes."

"If Jennifer would get organized in the morning she wouldn't have to yell at me," Sarah said happily.

Jack started up the stairs. He met Kate at the top of the stairwell. "If I'd known you were going to make it home on time, I could have slept in. It's your turn to get the little darlings ready for school."

"I've been up all night," Jack whispered. "I've got to get some sleep."

"You never help around the house. You should be taking those girls to school."

"I had a death last night. I don't feel up to discussing our relative contributions to the family."

"Just because some patient died is no reason to ignore your daughters. Every time something doesn't go your way you act all depressed. I'm sick of your weakness."

Jack laughed noiselessly and said, "It's the support of a loving family that makes everything worthwhile."

He walked into the bedroom, too tired to undress. He shut his eyes and tried to sleep. More yelling erupted downstairs. Jack stared at the ceiling. He couldn't shake the image of Bob's frightened eyes before he put him back to sleep to reintubate him. Bob never woke again. Then he visualized Bob lying underneath a white blanket in the recovery room after everything failed. Over and over Jack went over the case from beginning to end. Had he missed something? What had gone wrong? Could he have done anything to change the outcome?

Then the fear began. It grew and became sinister. Jack had cared for a patient, and now that patient was dead. It hadn't been some elderly patient undergoing a risky, but potentially life-saving, procedure. This patient was in the prime of life. The procedure was simple, something that seldom failed. Bob didn't have a bad heart or cancer. He hadn't been severely traumatized in an accident. He was young, and now he was dead.

Voyeuristic interest of doctors, nurses, and administrators was unavoidable, as was review of this case in the hospital morbidity and mortality conference. M&M conferences emboldened egotistical physicians with twenty-twenty hindsight to pontificate. Their conclusion was preordained. Since the attempted therapy failed, it must have been wrong. Dr. Jack Andrews shouldn't have intervened. Drs. Stevens and Walker should have continued by-the-book maneuvers. No one would admit there was no diagnosis to explain the reaction or why it continued despite all efforts. Their lack of diagnosis wouldn't stop them from condemning Jack.

Jack thought about the coming lawsuit. *How would the lawyers get involved? Who would call them? The family who hadn't shown up for the operation?* No use worrying about who would initiate the suit. A young man was dead, and Jack would need to defend himself.

Jack knew his colleagues—he found that characterization laughable—were even now redirecting blame away from themselves. He was the only physician present during the entire event. Lawyers couldn't win a case by claiming multiple people had each made a mistake and each individual mistake had contributed to a bad outcome. Lawyers required a single target, and he would be that target. He could defend himself, but the defense would be long and difficult. He didn't want to go through it.

Get hold of yourself, Jack thought. *You've spent your life in the operating room. You can handle this.* Even he found that thought hollow.

He couldn't sleep and gave up after two hours. The girls were in school and Kate was gone. He called his malpractice company to report the event.

The risk manager spoke reassuringly, "It sounds like you did nothing wrong, certainly nothing that qualifies as malpractice. These things happen, especially in the operating room. Most likely nothing will come of it. But, just to complete our file, could you send us a detailed letter about the occurrence? Within twenty-four hours. I'm not worried, but, you know, your malpractice policy mandates we collect information on any unusual event as soon as it happens. But don't worry. Just keep on practicing good medicine, and don't discuss anything about this case with anyone. Ever."

Jack, not reassured, spent the next two hours writing a detailed five-page letter to his malpractice insurance carrier. Nowhere in the letter did he offer an opinion or even an editorial comment. He wrote the letter as a consummate professional discussing an unfortunate event.

While composing the letter he again considered the upcoming, and almost certainly hostile, morbidity and mortality conference. Jack determined to describe precisely the patient's signs and symptoms and how he'd responded to them. He'd never speculate on the performance of other physicians. Most importantly, he'd never speak defensively. He knew any expression of self-defense made him look guilty. More to the point, it made him look weak. He must never appear weak. Weak people became targets.

The letter completed, Jack again tried to sleep. He couldn't close his eyes. He attempted to walk on the treadmill, but his legs were weak. He tried reading a novel and found he couldn't focus on the printed word. Finally, he settled in front of the television. Nothing good was on.

CHAPTER SIX

Kate and the girls returned around six o'clock. She immediately sent the children upstairs and then walked into the living room. She stood between Jack and the television. Her hands went to her hips. "You're going to work tomorrow, aren't you?"

"I think I'll take tomorrow off. It's a light week in the OR and they can get along without me."

Kate's voice was as hard as her face. "You act like a little girl. Want us all to feel sorry for you. Other doctors were involved in that case, and I bet they don't have to take two days off."

"I always appreciate your insight into the life of a physician."

"Every day off decreases the quarterly bonus you get from the anesthesia group. How am I supposed to raise a family when I'm married to someone as lazy as you?"

"Why don't you leave me alone and go shopping or something with your sophisticated and deep-thinking friends? You know, the doctors' wives."

Kate stormed out of the room.

Jack walked to the phone and called his anesthesia group administrator. "Look, I won't be in tomorrow or Friday either. Can you cover me?"

The administrator understood Dr. Andrews was making a statement, not requesting permission. "We can manage, I guess. Are you OK?"

"Sure. Just a little under the weather. See everyone back there on Monday."

Jack avoided Kate and said only a few words to his children during the next two days. He took a few walks around his backyard but didn't

37

venture away from his house. He didn't want to encounter anyone. Exhaustion finally induced sleep around eight o'clock Thursday evening. He slept like a dead man for fourteen hours.

The house was empty when he awoke. The girls were in school. He didn't care where Kate was.

Kate returned with the children after school and informed Jack that she and the girls were going out for pizza. She neglected to invite Jack.

This didn't surprise him, nor did it displease him.

CHAPTER SEVEN

J ack slept dreamlessly Friday night. He woke at 9:15 Saturday morning, showered, dressed, and joined the family in the kitchen. Kate greeted him with an icy glare.

Jennifer spoke up. "Dad, Sarah and I have soccer games this afternoon. Sarah plays at one, and I play at three. Can you come?"

"I wouldn't miss those games for the world. Shall we go out and have lunch before the games?"

Kate crossed her arms and growled, "I think I should just cook at home. There hasn't been much money coming in lately."

After bowls of soup and cold meat sandwiches, the family went together to the soccer field. Sarah spent her on-field time avoiding contact with other players while modeling her cute new soccer uniform. Jennifer approached the game differently. She played aggressively and intimidated her opponents. Kate and Jack sat together and talked to other parents, but not to each other. Kate spent most of the afternoon discussing how poorly Medicare reimbursed anesthesiologists. Jack and a couple of other bird hunters bemoaned the continued decrease in pheasant populations. Things were back to normal. His children practiced their skills of manipulation and his wife complained about money. There's nothing more secure than familiar territory

Jack returned to work Monday. He greeted fellow anesthesiologists as he changed into scrub clothes. His peers thoughtfully kept the small talk innocuous. Jack walked into the operating suite, checked the schedule, and went to the room assigned to him for the day, OR8.

After checking the anesthesia machine in OR8, Jack walked to the pharmacy to check out drugs for his first case. Ken Adams came up behind him and laid his hand on Jack's shoulder. Ken looked tentative. "I just wanted you to know the craniotomy patient from the other night did well."

"That's good. Thanks for your help."

Ken spoke quietly. "Look, I can't bill for that case. I was just being a Good Samaritan. I'll have the anesthesia group credit you for the case."

Jack, suddenly wary, said, "I can't bill for that case. I didn't finish it. Just go ahead and collect. I appreciated your help."

"I'll tell the group administrator to credit you," Dr. Adams insisted. "You interact with the administrator, decide how to handle the billing, how you want it entered in the group's record. I don't want anything more to do with it. Do what you think best."

Jack heard the pharmacist clear his throat. He turned away from Adams to find the drugs he needed laying on the counter before him. He nodded to the pharmacist and signed the paperwork. As he turned to walk to OR8 he said, "OK."

Ken spoke to Jack's back. "Really tough luck the other night."

Jack didn't turn around or slow his stride as he walked away.

That day, the next, and the next passed routinely. Jack did his cases. No one mentioned anything about the death in the OR, at least not in his presence. At first Jack tried to avoid any difficult case, any case with potential for complications. But it's impossible to predict such things. He realized he'd have to practice his profession and accept his and his patients' shared fates.

CHAPTER EIGHT

One month later Jack received a notice from hospital administration. The next morbidity and mortality conference would discuss his case. This was routine. A death had occurred in the OR. All such deaths were reviewed by hospital quality assurance and routed to the M&M conference.

Morbidity and mortality conferences are a universal exercise in all medical centers. These rounds feature frank discussion concerning what caused, or is thought to have caused, a particular patient's poor results and what should be done in the future to prevent such results from recurring. Supposedly such rounds are presented dispassionately in an effort to educate fellow physicians. Often, however, the rounds deteriorate into faultfinding and ego gratification by individuals who possess medical degrees but no empathy for their fellow physicians. There are no holds barred. Sometimes a physician appears before peers because of poor judgment or inept technical skills. More often, the physician is in the hot seat because he or she happened to be at the wrong place at the wrong time.

Jack and five other anesthesiologists attended this conference. Also present were two dozen surgeons from various subspecialties. Dr. Larry Walker stood at the podium, ready to present. Dr. Richard Madison, anesthesiologist and long-term chair of quality assurance, sat in the front row ready to take the notes necessary to prove the meeting had occurred. These notes were confidential and legally not discoverable. This ensured a free exchange of ideas without fear that opinions expressed could fall into the hands of malpractice attorneys.

Dr. Walker began by noting the date of surgery and the date of death. He characterized the patient, identified only by initials, as basically healthy. The operation was routine. He carefully noted that the patient did well in the immediate postoperative period. Subsequent to Dr. Walker completing his task, which he'd performed faultlessly, this patient suddenly experienced pulmonary edema. Dr. Walker didn't know what caused the pulmonary edema, but, in his experience, such complications were caused either by an overload of IV fluid or by heart failure.

Since it was not in Dr. Walker's area of expertise to administer IV fluids or to monitor the heart in the recovery room, he needed others to evaluate these possibilities.

Dr. Walker noted the usual methods had been attempted to control the symptoms. He didn't know if these therapeutic measures might have succeeded given enough time because an aggressive consultant forced him to attempt a radical trial of cardiopulmonary bypass. He'd finally agreed to this treatment only because of intense pressure this consultant placed on him. He wasn't aware this radical therapy had ever been successful in the past. In fact, he didn't believe anyone, anywhere, had attempted such therapy. The radical therapy failed and the patient expired.

Dr. Madison took off his glasses and carefully cleaned them with a small cloth carried expressly for such purpose. He made the gesture to convey his status as an exact and thoughtful man.

Jack couldn't stand Richard Madison. Madison had arrived on staff the same year Jack had. He was older than Jack, having spent a few years in the army prior to beginning his pursuit of fortune in the private world. He approached the practice of anesthesia with an inflated opinion of his medical skills and his personal virtue.

It had become immediately apparent Dr. Madison possessed neither the nerve nor the skills to take on difficult cases. The anesthesia group's schedulers recognized this, and he spent his career doing easy cases on healthy patients. This, at first, bruised Dr. Madison's ego. Recognizing what had happened, he began rationalizing that he had the practice he wanted because such a practice afforded him more time at home. He often spoke of how much he enjoyed domestic life and how he wasn't driven by the pursuit of money. Therefore he couldn't be expected to stay for those long, difficult cases that often occurred late in the day or at night.

Dr. Richard Madison was a coward.

The results of all this were predictable. First, he actually had few patients experience complications because he worked only in can't-miss situations. Second, he was resentful of anesthesiologists who possessed genuine skill.

Dr. Madison addressed the room. "I agree with Dr. Walker's two points. Life-threatening pulmonary edema is usually caused by an overload of intravenous fluid or by heart failure. And the treatment attempted was novel, to say the least. Some would even characterize it as without basis in medical literature. I think some explanation is due us. Perhaps Dr. Andrews, the anesthesiologist of record in this case, would enlighten us as to why he made this decision."

Jack, sitting in the second row, replied without standing. "Doctor, the patient did not die of isolated pulmonary edema. He died because he lost integrity of his entire vascular system. Only someone who hasn't thoroughly reviewed the chart would characterize this death as caused by an overload of IV fluid or heart failure. Either that, or the person coming to that conclusion doesn't possess a basic understanding of cardiovascular physiology."

"Doctor, I don't believe it's necessary to hang an exotic tag on this event," Madison replied defensively. "The patient undoubtedly suffered pulmonary edema. Pulmonary edema is due to heart failure. Either the heart itself fails and is unable to pump blood forward, or else the heart is confronted with more blood than it's designed to pump. The medical literature has well-established therapeutic modalities for treating this problem. There's no denying that. You deviated from standard medical principles. The patient is dead. What can you say to back up your position?"

Jack, his voice rising too much, said, "The two possibilities you're fixated on are disproved by even a cursory review of the chart. If the patient had suffered from an overload of fluid, his blood pressure would have been high, very high. In fact, the overwhelming problem we faced in caring for this patient was low blood pressure unresponsive to any therapy. Secondly, multiple people monitored the EKG throughout the entire episode. No one saw any change consistent with a heart problem. Is it too much to ask the chair of the quality assurance committee to actually put some thought into this review?"

"I did review the chart," Madison fired back. "Personal attacks won't change the result for this patient. Even if something unusual was going on, the fact is you carried out a course of action unsupported in conventional medicine."

Jack forced himself to gain control. "Dr. Walker and the consultant he chose, Dr. Stevens, carried out the usual maneuvers. Everything they did, everything classically taught, failed. If this had been what we usually see, their therapy would have worked. The fact nothing worked demonstrates something out of the ordinary occurred."

Madison, feigning incredulity, said, "So, what happened, Doctor?"

"The patient experienced some sort of allergic reaction. His vascular system became porous and couldn't perfuse the body. The process was irreversible."

"Doctor, you say it was an allergic reaction. Did you treat him for such a reaction?"

"The patient received the usual treatment for an allergic reaction, such as Benadryl, epinephrine, and steroids. But the reaction was massive and nothing worked."

Madison was smug. "What do you suppose caused the problem? Did you administer a drug you shouldn't have?"

"Even a short chart review demonstrates the patient didn't receive any drugs he hadn't been exposed to in the past. I believe he most likely reacted to something in one of the transfused units of blood. This would account for the magnitude of the reaction. Another possibility is he reacted to latex. He was exposed to latex in the surgeon's gloves and also in the Foley catheter."

Gloating, Madison declared, "Whatever the cause was, the patient died of pulmonary edema, and the therapy was not what is recommended."

"He didn't die of pulmonary edema. The record clearly shows his oxygen saturation never fell to life-threatening levels. Your diagnosis of the cause of death demonstrates ignorance of what happened."

"No matter what you say, you deviated from the usual methodology. I'd never treat a patient with such serious problems the way you did."

Jack looked directly into Richard Madison's eyes. "When was the last time anyone asked you to treat a patient with a serious problem?"

An angry Richard Madison carefully studied his watch. "It's seven fifteen and we have to end this discussion. I'm sure we'll revisit this case in the future. Or at least some of us will."

Jack stood up. He felt Harry Herbert's hand on his shoulder. Harry seemed amused. "I guess you and good old Dick Madison won't be having each other over for Sunday dinner anytime soon."

"Sometimes it's impossible to be honest without being rude. I can't stand that asshole."

Harry replied with gentleness, "You did everything you could for your patient. You can't let someone who never cares for sick people make you second-guess yourself."

"Thanks, Harry. But one thing Madison said is true. I'll hear about this again."

CHAPTER NINE

Life went on for Dr. Jack Andrews. He performed well in the operating room. The only obvious change was his need to confer with consultants anytime a patient presented unexpected symptoms. The old hands in the operating room noticed this loss of self-confidence, this need to be reassured. They believed after a few months Jack would become less gun-shy and revert to his usual routine. And they were right. Jack's self-consciousness and self-pity faded over time. To the casual observer everything was back to normal.

Jack kept himself busy at all times. A moment of idleness became a moment to relive the case. He didn't sleep well, so late into every night he read medical journals and anything else he found interesting. He concentrated on history, philosophy, or technical subjects. Light reading wasn't for him. Light reading allowed his mind to wander.

Jack was also a hunter. He found he could, at least for a few hours, forget the pressures of life when he hunted, or planned a hunt, or practiced the exceptional shooting skills he'd developed during his formative years on the farm. In the rural environment of his youth hunting and other outdoor activities were the norm. He rather enjoyed the fact his urban acquaintances rejected hunting. Jack had spent his life since age eighteen pursuing a career in medicine. He'd labored to join the club of self-declared elites who considered themselves more sophisticated and intelligent than anyone else in society. Medicine is a discipline of tradition, regulation, and large egos. Its practitioners are expected to play by the rules. Jack enjoyed hunting all the more because it induced disapproval among the politically correct and liberal people who shared his profession.

At home nothing changed. Jennifer and Sarah regarded their privileged lifestyle as an entitlement. Theirs was the perfect urban existence, and they never considered how it came about. They were certain all good things came from their mother. Their father was a peripheral figure, easily manipulated when they wanted something, but otherwise of little impact in their lives.

Kate was relieved when Jack lost only a couple of days' work due to his depression over a patient's death. His depression over a bad outcome symbolized weakness. Jack had many weaknesses, and Kate was pleased she'd learned to exploit so many of them. His major weakness was, of course, the children. Kate knew the children gave her a decisive edge in any marital conflict.

Jack's other major weakness was money. He'd grown up in a family with a tight budget. The thought of returning to that state frightened him. Kate knew divorce, with its attendant financial consequences, was something Jack dreaded.

Kate knew Jack was a valuable and manageable resource. Controlling her husband had become almost too easy.

CHAPTER TEN

Over the next few months Jack worked harder. He found it easier to put in more hours than listen to Kate's complaints about how much more money other physicians made. Incomes were, it seemed, her only serious topic of conversation.

Each day after work Jack went into Kate-avoidance mode. He traveled straight to a health club, where he ran, lifted weights, rode an exercise bike, or climbed stairs until physically exhausted. He neither required nor desired a personal trainer or exercise partner. His five-foot-ten-inch frame carried two hundred pudgy pounds on the day Bob died. He'd looked like a former athlete beginning the gradual slide into middle age. After three months in the gym he dropped twenty pounds. His face grew thinner and frown lines appeared for the first time. Four months into his new physical regimen he looked into the mirror at his still-dark brown hair, cut short to fit under an operating room hat. He thought, *fuck this*, and quit worrying about haircuts.

Every night he returned home late, found leftovers in the refrigerator, heated them in the microwave oven, and ate at the kitchen table alone. He always checked in the inappropriately named family room to see if either of his daughters was interested in conversation. Mostly they weren't.

Then Jack retired to his study to read, or if he were unusually tired, watch television. An hour or two later, he'd go to bed, and, making sure he didn't disturb Kate, fall asleep almost immediately. An alarm clock bleated five or six hours later and announced the beginning of another cycle.

On free weekends he visited a local shooting range. Exceptional marksmen share a common trait: when on the trigger nothing distracts them. Nothing in their personal or professional life matters. Their emotional state doesn't matter. Conversation at the adjacent shooting bench doesn't matter. Nothing matters except concentration on the sight and the execution of perfect mechanics in pressing the trigger so the sight never comes off target as the weapon discharges. Thoughts of the consequence of the shot have been considered and accepted. The shooter is beyond thought. For an instant, the individual becomes the weapon. In that moment the true marksman achieves a level of focus unknown in usual human endeavors. The shooter knows how rare this achievement is and strives to recapture the feeling again and again.

Jack lived for those moments.

CHAPTER ELEVEN

One year after Bob's death, Jack received a call from Richard Madison. As chair of the quality assurance committee, Dr. Madison was routinely made aware of any request for review of a medical record. With barely concealed glee Madison said, "There's a lawyer looking into a case in which a patient died after routine surgery. He was really aggressive with the medical records staff and was especially interested in the novel therapy administered for the treatment of pulmonary edema. But I guess that's par for the course for a guy who only accepts a case when he's sure he'll win big money. And this guy always wins big money. Anyway, it's a case you know well. Just thought I'd call you as a professional courtesy."

"I really want to thank you," Jack replied sarcastically. "You're exhibiting your usual level of professionalism. It's marvelous to talk to someone like you, a person who so enjoys his work."

A week later the hospital operator paged Jack. The operator asked if he would accept an outside call. Jack agreed. The voice on the line belonged to a young female. "Hello, is this Dr. Jack Andrews?"

Her tone was formal. Jack could hear his own heart beating. "Yes, this is Dr. Andrews. What can I do for you?"

"My name is Connie Morton. I'm a paralegal with Mr. Carl Hafen. He asked me to schedule a deposition with you."

Jack took a deep breath. "May I ask what this is about?"

The voice became vague, practiced. "I'm not directed to discuss that with you. Would you have your attorney contact Mr. Hafen's office at 633-5267 to set up the deposition?"

Jack tried to sound nonchalant. "Sure."

He heard an immediate click.

Jack thought, *I'll have to get a fucking lawyer. Do these guys know I don't even have a lawyer?* He felt sick and scared, but the most overwhelming emotion he experienced was guilt. Like most physicians, Jack regarded himself as one of the elite. He'd always been at the top of any class he'd taken and had flown through medical school and residency. He passed his boards in anesthesiology on the first try. He was used to being treated as someone special, at least when he wasn't home. Now he'd been commanded to report to an attorney's office. He felt like a criminal.

Jack knew he had no control over events and this frightened him to his soul. In truth, he knew he could never be an effective criminal. And he was sure he'd be even worse as a defendant.

Jack thought about things for fifteen minutes. Then he called his malpractice insurance carrier to report his need for an attorney.

A secretary answered and confirmed he was insured by her employer. Jack told her his problem. She told him to hang on while she transferred his call to a claims representative.

While on hold Jack listened to classical music on National Public Radio, music intended to be restful. It wasn't. Jack involuntarily jumped as he was connected. "Hello, Dr. Andrews, this is Peggy Jackson. I'm a claims representative. What can I do for you?"

"I've been notified an attorney named Carl Hafen wants to depose me," Jack answered. "I suspect it's about a case I did last year."

"Yes, I have your letter regarding that case before me now." Peggy Jackson was utterly professional. "We looked at your letter and concluded there was no basis for a claim against you."

Jack attempted to sound equally professional. "Well, there's nothing else in my life that would trigger a deposition."

"All right, Doctor, I'll tell you what's going to happen. There are several defense lawyers we consult. We'll have one of them call Mr. Hafen's office and find out what's going on." Peggy Jackson's soft feminine voice expressed an undercurrent of toughness.

"Thanks, Ms. Jackson. They gave me the phone number for Hafen's office."

"That's OK, Doctor. We have his office number. That particular individual is well known to us. Now I want to remind you of some very basic things. You're not to discuss this case with anyone, anyone at all. Second, stay away from the patient's hospital record. Don't go to medical records, don't reread any part of the chart, don't touch that record. Lastly, communication regarding this case will be handled only through this office or through the attorney's office we designate. If you violate any of these conditions, it may make it impossible for us to defend you. Do you understand?"

"I understand."

"And, Doctor, try not to take any of this personally. Anyone can sue anyone for anything in this country. Being named in a legal action doesn't demonstrate proof of negligence or guilt. Keep practicing good medicine. Don't let this affect your personal life. This action shouldn't be allowed to affect your self-image as a physician. Always remember this is only about money."

"Thank you for your concern, Ms. Jackson. I'll wait to hear from you."

"Very good, Doctor. We'll be in touch."

Peggy Jackson felt uncomfortable as she hung up the phone. This guy sounded too unsure. He might be the kind of guy Carl Hafen could bust up.

Time would tell.

CHAPTER TWELVE

Two days later Jack received a call. "Hello, Dr. Andrews? This is Ben Harris. I'm the attorney your insurer retained for the upcoming deposition. Peggy Jackson asked me to give you a call."

"Thank you, Mr. Harris. I've never been through anything like this, and I could use all the guidance you can offer."

"I'm here to help. The subject of contention involves one Robert Parker, a patient who died after routine surgery for gastrointestinal bleeding. I'm sure you're able to recall the case."

"I remember it."

"Thought so. The deposition will be held in my office ten days from now, the sixteenth at 2:00 p.m."

"How should I prepare?"

"Well, you should go over the patient record and be fully conversant with everything that occurred during the entire hospitalization. Since you're unable to access the actual patient chart my office will FedEx a copy to you. You should also brush up on recent medical literature that supports your position, which is, of course, that the care you offered Mr. Parker was appropriate and up to national standards."

"Shouldn't we meet so you can educate me about the process and how I should answer questions?"

"Don't worry, Doctor. I've handled many cases of alleged professional malpractice in the past. I'll be there every step of the way. Why don't you come to my office one hour prior to the deposition? We'll go over the rules then."

"That's enough time?"

"Doctor, I do this for a living. It'll be plenty of time. Look, I'm due in court in just a few minutes. Just remember, if you require anything, anything at all, call my secretary. We're always there for you."

Jack slowly put the phone back into the cradle. His life was out of control, and the only thing protecting him was a legal robot that had other, more important things, on his mind.

CHAPTER THIRTEEN

Jack spent every possible minute preparing for the deposition. His actions throughout the case were imprinted in his memory; he didn't require a chart review to know what he'd seen and how he'd responded. It was, however, necessary he review every entry on the record. It was inevitable there were comments on the chart made by nurses or doctors who disagreed with the diagnosis or the treatment. These comments might be slightly disparaging or frankly hostile. Jack prepared to refute all such opinions.

Until the copy of the chart arrived, Jack studied all relevant medical literature relating to Bob Parker's medical condition.

Every evening immediately after his workout and evening meal, Jack went to his home office, shut the door, and reviewed pulmonary edema, blood transfusions, allergic reactions, low blood pressure, and heart failure. On deposition day he couldn't afford to appear incompetent and he didn't want to be surprised.

On the fourth night, an angry Kate threw the door open. "What the hell do you do up here every night?"

Jack, amazed Kate wanted to talk about anything other than money, was nonplussed by her sudden appearance. "As you know, dear, next week there's a deposition concerning the death I had last year. I'm preparing for it."

Kate responded coldly, "I don't know why you worry so much about that. You have malpractice insurance. Just let them pay off so you can get back to work full-time."

"That's not the way it works, Kate. Now that I've been sued, even if I win, I have to list that case on every future application I make for hospital privileges, malpractice insurance, and Medicare provider information…forever. If I lose, I'll look even worse. And I have a limit of one million dollars on my malpractice policy. You remember when I wanted to pay more for a higher limit? You raised such hell about the expense I didn't buy it. Now what do you suppose will happen if I lose and the jury awards this guy's family more than a million? Who do you suppose is going to pay the difference? It will adversely affect your lifestyle, to say the least."

"If they get more than a million, we'll just hide our money and declare bankruptcy. They can't touch us personally."

"What an original concept…do you have any idea what bullshit that is?"

"Don't make fun of me."

"Well, dear, I've got to tell you, you're wrong. Dead wrong. Doctors aren't allowed to declare bankruptcy to duck legal judgments. We're expected to work our way out of debt. And besides, how are we going to hide our money? Have you perfected some sort of offshore account? I'm sure the lawyers would love it if they found a money trail out of the country. It would be an admission of guilt."

"I'm sure you'll win if you pick up your balls and try for once to be tough. You better not let anyone push you around."

"You talk like an expert on life. How is that possible when your only real work experience is making sure your husband provides enough money so you can live in the manner you think you deserve?"

"Oh, sure, mock me. Remember, Jack, I do take care of your children. How long will the trial take?"

"About three or four weeks."

"You can't be expected to miss that much work. We have no income if you aren't working. You'll just have to make the lawyers attend the trial. There's no reason you have to be there all the time."

"Gee, honey, I think it's expected I show up for my own trial."

"It isn't fair. Why should the children and I have to suffer just because some guy had a poor result?"

"Dying is a very poor result."

"You just aren't tough enough, are you? I can't believe I'm supposed to raise children with someone who isn't strong and has all these problems."

"Life really isn't fair, is it, Kate?"

Kate slammed the door as she stalked out of the room. Jack thought it remarkable a door could make that much noise and remain on its hinges.

CHAPTER FOURTEEN

The day of the deposition was bright and sunny. Jack arranged to take the entire day off work, much to Kate's dismay. She felt it only reasonable that Jack earn at least a little money before noon as partial recompense for his many failings. Jack got up later than usual, showered, and put on the suit he rarely wore. He planned to stop downtown for a bite to eat prior to the deposition in the hope some food might settle his stomach.

Kate was waiting when Jack came down the stairs. "I just want you to know I can't believe I'm married to someone like you. What kind of father would lead his family into this kind of trouble?"

"Kate, thanks for your concern. It gives me strength to know how supportive you are when times get tough. I know you'll be with me no matter what happens."

Jack found a coffee shop in a downtown hotel and tried to eat. After pushing his food around for fifteen minutes, he gave up. He drank a couple of Cokes and walked the two blocks to Ben Harris's office.

Jack walked through the doorway at five minutes to one. The office was furnished in unimaginative twentieth century American style. Jack guessed it was supposed to convey an impression of efficiency. The twenty-five-or-so-year-old woman behind the receptionist desk wore too much makeup and too much jewelry, an apparent attempt to look pert and stylish. "Hello, my name is Holly. What can I do for you?" She gave Jack one of those fake smiles teenage girls affect when posing for a group picture at some silly high school event.

"My name is Jack Andrews. I'm here to see Mr. Harris. I've got an appointment at one o'clock."

"Mr. Harris won't be here until one thirty. He sends his apologies. He had an unavoidable conflict."

"How's this going to work? Mr. Harris intended to coach me prior to my deposition at two. Is the deposition going to be delayed?"

"Mr. Harris wanted you to know the deposition will still take place at two. He feels there will be plenty of time to talk prior to the deposition. There's really not much to discuss."

"Does he know I've never been to a deposition before?"

"Don't worry, Dr. Andrews. Everything will be fine. Please sit down. Relax. Read a magazine."

The magazines didn't interest Jack—they were all about money management or golf. Jack thought he'd soon have no money to manage, which in turn made it unlikely he'd join any country clubs. Obviously Harris had no overwhelming interest in Jack's problem. Jack wondered why his malpractice company had retained this guy. Were they going to make a deal to cut losses as soon as possible? Was Jack destined for sacrifice?

Ben Harris swept into his office at 1:40. He wore a gray pinstripe suit that might have looked better had no paunch been hanging over the belt. He was probably in his mid-forties, although booze and cigarettes were hurrying the aging process. His gray hair was long in an attempt at sophistication, his complexion florid.

Harris had the look of a used car salesman twenty minutes late for work.

There was a short, quiet conversation between Harris and Holly. She periodically nodded toward Jack. The attorney turned around. "Dr. Andrews, so glad to meet you. Why don't you step into my office? Would you like a cup of coffee?"

Jack made no attempt to hide his disgust. "What I would like is some instruction on what a deposition entails. Perhaps you'd consent to be my legal advisor. That is, unless you're too busy at the moment."

The attorney looked distressed. "Dr. Andrews, please step into my office. We have some things to discuss."

He ushered Jack into an office lined with bookshelves. Jack didn't believe many of the books had actually been read. Harris sat down behind his desk, rolled his chair forward, and addressed Jack in his best professional baritone. "Dr. Andrews, don't let the process upset you. I can assure you a deposition is a routine matter. All you have to do is tell the truth, but don't elaborate on any point. Just give short, direct answers. I won't let the opposing attorney lead you anywhere you shouldn't go. Don't worry. I do this all the time."

Jack stared into his representative's eyes. "I don't do this all the time. You indicated it was of utmost importance we meet for an hour prior to the deposition to prepare me. Now it's ten minutes until we begin and all you can say is preparation is no big deal. Tell me, which set of instructions is correct?"

"Dr. Andrews, I'm sorry we've gotten off on the wrong foot," Harris replied. "I can assure you I have your best interests at heart. I'm truly sorry I was detained this afternoon, but the deposition must take place at the appointed hour. We would inconvenience too many people if we attempted to delay the process."

"I certainly wouldn't want to inconvenience any members of your profession while they play games with my life. Now explain to me why it's so important we go now. After all, you people have waited months to get this thing off the ground."

"Doctor, you're overreacting to this. It takes months to set up a deposition because it involves so many busy people. Just answer the questions in a straightforward manner. Don't editorialize on anything. I really don't believe they have a case."

"Have you actually read the medical record?"

"Doctor, I read everything your malpractice company highlighted in the record. I could hardly afford the time to go through a voluminous medical record simply to prepare for a short deposition. Now let's go to the conference room and get started. Remember, your malpractice insurance contract specifies the company is in charge of your defense. If they aren't allowed to make appropriate decisions, your policy is null and void. They have retained me to direct you during this deposition. I'll do my job. Just remember what I told you in regard to answering questions."

Ben Harris rose heavily from his chair and lumbered to the door. Jack followed, his feelings of dread now replaced with feelings of hopelessness.

CHAPTER FIFTEEN

arl Hafen, already seated on the side of the conference table away from the door, appraised the two men entering the room. He knew Ben Harris well. Harris understood the game. On occasion he performed competently, but he was incapable of anything resembling imagination or cleverness. He'd give the malpractice company an evaluation based on the cost of settling the case versus the cost of defending it. The merits of the case never entered into the cost analysis. When the time came, Harris would make the deal.

Hafen then regarded Dr. Jack Andrews with the dispassionate attitude of a predator selecting a victim. Hafen had much experience litigating medical malpractice cases. He knew it possible to confuse a carefully selected jury with medical jargon. Then their decision had to be based simply on which of the opponents they liked best. What Carl Hafen needed to win was a physician defendant who projected one of two possible deficiencies. He required either a physician who was arrogant and conceited or a physician who was defensive and unsure of himself.

This guy, Dr. Jack Andrews, looked depressed and worried. Excellent. Hafen planned to ask questions during the deposition to ensure his instincts were correct.

Hafen rose from his chair and reached across the table to shake hands with Ben Harris. The men contrasted sharply. Hafen exercised regularly to keep a slim figure. His brown hair was cut to appear professional without a hint of personal vanity. His suit was well cut, but not extravagant. His wire-rimmed glasses would look natural on a thoughtful college professor. The look conveyed to a jury that this was a man who sought justice, not personal aggrandizement. Law was a high-stakes game, and a contestant must seize every advantage.

Hafen noted, as he shook hands with the doctor, the lack of direct eye contact. His movements were stiff; he looked woefully out of place. Carl Hafen was pleased.

Hafen employed a young secretary in his office who did some filing and occasionally answered the phone. She possessed one real asset. Her equally young husband was working his way through college with a night job cleaning operating rooms in the city's largest hospital. The young man didn't broadcast where his wife worked. He'd become helpful in providing background information on hospital personnel. He couldn't glean much useful medical information, but his knowledge of personalities often revealed personal weaknesses a clever attorney could exploit. Carl Hafen was very clever.

The young man knew this doctor. He told Hafen that Dr. Andrews was polite and cared about his patients. Andrews often seemed unusually tired and sad, if not downright depressed. Gossip around the hospital indicated the doctor had a high-maintenance wife. Rumors suggested he spent an extraordinary amount of time in the operating room to earn money for her upkeep, and, more importantly, to stay away from her. Carl Hafen appreciated the insight. He hoped Andrews might be near his breaking point.

The deposition began with the usual statements of time and place, followed by a promise to tell the truth. That is, the witness had to tell the truth. The lawyers promised nothing. Hafen recited the routine questions and established Jack Andrews did indeed possess a medical degree, had completed a residency in anesthesia, and had been certified by the American Board of Anesthesiology.

Carl Hafen then leaned across the table, looked directly into Jack's eyes, and asked the most carefully prepared question of the deposition: "Dr. Andrews, on the evening in question, isn't it true you left your patient, Robert Parker, in the recovery room and proceeded to start another case?"

Jack had never considered his proceeding with an emergency case, especially a craniotomy, for God's sake, would be an issue. He was floored by the question's implication that he had deliberately abandoned the care of Robert Parker.

"Well, yes, I guess that's true. I was on call and there was an emergency craniotomy to do."

Hafen leaned in closer to Jack. "Is it the standard of care, Doctor, to leave a patient in critical condition and proceed to another operation?" The word *doctor* was pronounced in a pejorative tone of voice.

Pangs of guilt assaulted Jack. Had his beginning another case somehow caused the death of Robert Parker? This had not occurred to him before. He struggled to control his emotions. His self-confidence went from low to nonexistent. "Well, the patient, Robert Parker, appeared stable at the time we went on to our next case. There was no reason to delay the craniotomy."

"Doctor, is it not true there was a physician on second call that night?"

"There's always someone on second call."

"Now, the biggest disadvantage to you personally for calling in the second-call anesthesiologist would be that you then wouldn't receive the fee for performing anesthesia for the craniotomy. Isn't that true, Doctor?"

"I never let the fee for performing anesthesia influence my decision-making when caring for patients."

"How much is the fee for performing anesthesia for a craniotomy, Doctor?"

"I suppose it would range from one thousand to fifteen hundred dollars."

"That's a lot of money. You have a nice house, a nice car; your wife doesn't work. It takes a lot of money to maintain that lifestyle, doesn't it, Doctor?"

Jack looked to his right for help from Ben Harris. Harris slowly roused himself. "Mr. Hafen, this deposition has the purpose of discovering facts concerning a particular medical case. The doctor's lifestyle is not the issue."

Hafen, looking like a cat that knows where the mouse is hiding, went on. "OK, we'll drop that line of questioning, for now. But I'd like to know one more thing, Doctor. Who actually billed for the performance of anesthesia on the craniotomy patient?"

"No one billed for the craniotomy."

"That's surprising, Doctor. After all, the fee for that operation is substantial. Why was no bill submitted?"

"I didn't bill because I called the second-call anesthesiologist to take over that case when Mr. Parker began having difficulty. Dr. Adams, who took over the case for me, didn't bill because he wasn't present for the whole case."

"Are you sure that's the reason Dr. Adams didn't bill for the case?"

"I guess you'll have to ask him about that."

"Oh, I will, Doctor. Rest assured. But I have another theory. It might be that neither of you billed for that case because things were not up to the standard of care that night. Maybe both of you have something to be ashamed of concerning your actions regarding Robert Parker and the craniotomy patient."

Jack again turned to Ben Harris. Mr. Harris seemed fascinated by something he was watching through the window.

"Doctor, why do you believe Mr. Parker died?"

"I believe he died of an allergic reaction."

"An original thought, Doctor. What do you think caused the reaction? After all, if you believe your patient died of an allergic reaction you must have identified some specific agent."

"I believe he died due to a reaction to something in one of the units of transfused blood."

"Isn't it true, Doctor, that all units of blood were fully typed and cross matched prior to transfusion?"

"Of course. But that doesn't mean there couldn't have been something in one of them that initiated an allergic reaction."

"You're reaching, Doctor. Isn't it true Mr. Parker died of pulmonary edema? Simply put, he died of fluid in the lungs."

"Pulmonary edema was only one manifestation of his problems. What really happened was the patient lost all vascular integrity. He was leaking fluid from his entire vascular tree."

"Doctor, the patient, Robert Parker, experienced pulmonary edema. It's written all over the chart. Isn't it more likely you simply overloaded Mr. Parker with fluid and caused him to go into pulmonary edema? Isn't it a fact you caused him to drown in the excess fluid you administered? Isn't it true that pulmonary edema caused by your negligence resulted in the death of Robert Parker?"

"He did not die of fluid overload. He died—"

Hafen cut Jack off. "He not only died of pulmonary edema, but therapy for the problem was begun too late because you were off doing another case to earn more money. And then, to compound your negligence, you set off on some wild radical therapeutic regimen that has never been mentioned in the medical literature. Isn't that correct, Dr. Andrews?"

"That's not true. We tried everything we could to keep the patient alive."

"Why did you not listen to the advice of Mr. Parker's primary physician, Doctor? Why did you not allow the consultant in pulmonary medicine to continue the correct therapeutic maneuvers?"

"We did what we did because the standard therapy wasn't working."

"Doctor, I've deposed the surgeon on the case, the primary physician for Mr. Parker, Dr. Larry Walker. You know Dr. Walker, don't you?"

"Of course I know Dr. Walker." Jack wanted to end the sentence by saying "the dumb SOB."

"Dr. Walker feels differently about the case than you do."

Jack experienced an epiphany. He'd been sold out. Larry Walker had delivered him to Carl Hafen, attorney-at-law. Jack understood Larry Walker needed to provide the legal system with a single target so the surgeon wouldn't be forced to surrender any valuable money-generating time to the distasteful chore of defending another physician. It was more efficient to simply hand over a colleague. And safer.

The deposition went on for another hour. Hafen made Jack feel like a bewildered child. An incompetent, bewildered child.

Hafen was satisfied with the deposition. The facts were not key. In reality, the facts were nearly irrelevant. Dr. Andrews was unsure of himself and felt guilty about the patient's death. He wasn't terribly articulate. He was depressed. Dr. Jack Andrews was the perfect target.

Hafen said, "I think we have enough for today, Doctor. Unless your counsel has some questions I suggest we end the deposition."

Harris had no questions and agreed the process was over. He leaned over the table and shook Hafen's hand. They spoke a few words in low tones. Jack wasn't interested enough to try to understand their discussion. Then Hafen straightened up and strode out the door. The court recorder followed. Jack and his counsel were alone.

CHAPTER SIXTEEN

Jack looked up to make certain the office door was closed. He felt he should be angry because he'd received no legal representation, none at all. But he was too exhausted to summon up even the emotion of anger. Still staring at the floor, Jack said in a voice sounding monotone even to himself, "What happens next?"

"You have to know this isn't going to end anytime soon," Harris answered in a professional, sympathetic voice. "The process will continue."

"The process," Jack mused. "You make it sound as if it were some sterile procedure that always dispenses justice."

Attempting to reassert himself as a legal professional and captain of this ship, albeit a leaky ship, Harris said, "Doctor, everyone in the system is concerned with justice. It's just that the definition of justice is not the same for everyone involved."

Jack continued to stare at the floor. "You're better than I thought. I wouldn't have believed you could deliver that line with a straight face."

Harris tried to control his client. "Doctor, you're involved in a case that ended with a bad result. Get used to the fact that now it's just about money. That's the way it is for the dead guy's family, and for Carl Hafen, and for your insurance carrier. In this country justice is equated with money. I really don't care if you did or did not do the right thing in this case. I don't care. I'm here to do whatever is best for my client, who happens to be your malpractice insurer. It's how the game is played."

Jack looked straight into Harris's eyes. His voice sounded like it belonged to someone else. "Remember, counselor, it's just a game to you, but you and your friends are playing with my life."

Harris kept his game face. "Doctor, as we discussed earlier, your insurer is in charge of your defense. If you deviate from their advice, they can drop you."

A humorless smile crossed Jack's face. "I wonder how they'll feel after I discuss how well you prepared me for the deposition. And then they'll get a transcript of this deposition. They'll look in vain for evidence of your jumping in when I needed you to defend me. What you need to do now is to call the malpractice company and recommend they find me a new attorney. If you all agree it's in everyone's best interest to find me other representation, I'll keep my mouth shut about what happened here today."

Harris furiously hoped this son of a bitch went down big time. He also knew he had no choice but to go along. "All right. But you're making a big mistake. The people in the company's risk management section don't like their judgment questioned, especially by some doctor who's going to cost them a lot of money."

Jack stood up and stared down at the still seated attorney. "Make the call, counselor."

He walked out of the conference room, down the hall, and out the office door. He didn't acknowledge anyone as he left. He was trapped. His malpractice policy insured him for too little. His so-called colleagues at the hospital were in the process of isolating him as the single scapegoat. And apparently no one at the malpractice company thought it important to find him a good lawyer.

Everything he'd worked for his entire life, including his reputation, was about to be lost.

His clearest thought was that his enemies had made a fatal mistake when they left him with nothing left to lose.

CHAPTER SEVENTEEN

Harris punched in the phone number he knew from memory and asked for Peggy Jackson in the risk management section. She was awaiting his report and picked up immediately. "Hello, Ben. How'd things go?"

"Peggy, we have a problem with this doctor. Carl Hafen carved him up today. This guy won't look good in front of a jury and he won't take advice from his attorney. He's demanding a new lawyer."

Jackson knew Ben Harris well enough to be suspicious. "What's the problem between you two?"

Disdain in his voice, Harris said, "He blames me for not nurse-maiding him through the deposition. He thinks I should give him magic advice on how to answer Hafen's questions. I told him exactly what to do and how to behave. I really don't understand what he has to complain about."

"Ben, how much preparation did he get from you for this deposition?"

"We brought him to the office an hour ahead of time to discuss things. I was unavoidably detained, so he didn't get the whole hour."

"How much time did he get?"

"Maybe ten or fifteen minutes."

"Ben, perhaps knowing your client had never been deposed before you should have devoted a little more time to him."

"Look, Peggy, his preparation wasn't that important. Carl Hafen has a guy who died following surgery. He'll want a deal and so will we."

"Ben, Ben, Ben, do you think it's possible Hafen might deal more reasonably if he thought he might lose should the case go to trial?"

"Come on, Peggy. The dead guy was an unemployed drunk. He's not worth enough for Hafen to spend a month in court. He'll deal."

"Perhaps the doctor thinks he's in the right and wants vindication."

"Peggy, I can't believe I have to listen to such crap from you."

Jackson made up her mind. "If the doctor wants a new lawyer we'll get him one. As a gesture of goodwill to our client. We might secure a better deal if the doctor's more confident. I'll find someone else and have him or her contact your office for the relevant records. And, Ben, don't charge this office for the ten minutes you spent preparing for this deposition."

Harris unsuccessfully tried to keep the anger out of his voice. "Of course not. I'll get everything ready for the doctor's next attorney."

Jackson carefully replaced the phone back on the receiver. Harris was back to his old habits. He must have fallen off the wagon again. It was really too bad. The guy had once been a competent defense attorney. In spite of herself Peggy had to smile about one thing. This Dr. Andrews actually demonstrated decent judgment when he asked for a new attorney—most unusual for a physician.

CHAPTER EIGHTEEN

Jack drove home on autopilot. He parked the car in the garage and opened the door to the house. Kate blocked his way. "Another day with no work. I don't know why you didn't tell those lawyers to schedule this deposition in the evening or on a Saturday. Your time is much too valuable to waste answering stupid questions. Those lawyers made money today. You didn't."

It suddenly became clear to Jack that Kate's relentless greed had caused her to inhabit a world that had nothing to do with reality. He took it for granted she was willing to use him, but he'd supposed she existed in the real world. Now he recognized how mistaken he'd been. "I'll tell you what, Kate—this isn't just some lawyer trying to extort a few bucks. This is serious. I won't try to describe the atmosphere during the deposition, but my opponent can smell blood. And you can bet in court he'll ask for a lot more than a million dollars. Remember when you insisted the payout limit for a malpractice policy limit wasn't important? Because you somehow believed no plaintiff ever got more than the limit of the policy? Well, if someone has assets, lawyers will go after everything. Just another example of your shitty judgment. At least I'll have the satisfaction of seeing you go down with me."

Kate tried to sound defiant. "Screw them."

"My opponents are just like *you*. They'll be attached to my salary forever."

"What will happen to me?" There was a long pause. "And the children?"

Jack looked hard into Kate's eyes. "Maybe we should get divorced. I won't contest giving you the bulk of what we've acquired. I'm no lawyer, but maybe the other side can't touch child support. Maybe you can get away with enough money to support yourself until you seduce your next male target."

Kate shrieked, "I knew you were weak. I knew you'd let us down. You've never had what it takes to make it."

Jack was already on the stairway leading to his office. "Make your decision soon."

CHAPTER NINETEEN

The next day, Jack received a page for an outside call. He picked up and recognized Peggy Jackson's voice on the line. "Dr. Andrews, I'll get right to the point. I understand you and Ben Harris don't see eye to eye. Would you be more comfortable if we retained another attorney to represent you—and us—in this matter?"

Jack's voice had an edge. "That's a fine idea. I wonder if you can find an attorney who might actually read the medical record. It would also be nice to have some preparation before the next go around."

Peggy put on her warmest southern voice. "We have another attorney in mind. He's young and energetic. He's trying to make a name for himself."

"Does that mean he doesn't drink too much?"

"Doctor, we'll retain him. His name is Jon Olsen. He's a Midwesterner, just like you. We think you two will be comfortable with each other. He'll obtain the relevant records from Ben Harris's office. How does that sound?"

"Do I have a choice?"

"No. But I want to assure you I put a lot of thought into getting you more compatible representation."

"OK."

"It'll take Jon a little time to come up to speed on this matter. I think you need to get away from this for a while. Take some time off, maybe go on a trip. We'll have plenty of time for preparation when you get back."

Jack wondered if she really believed he could just go away and forget the case. It was as if Peggy Jackson believed being accused of a crime, which was what a malpractice claim was in Jack's mind, was just some minor inconvenience. "I'll check with you in two or three weeks."

CHAPTER TWENTY

One week later, Jack walked through the doorway into his house after his workout. Kate met him at the door, an unusual gesture. Behind her, Jack saw Sarah and Jennifer hurrying up the stairs. At the top of the stairway they both looked over their shoulders at Jack, then disappeared around the corner.

Kate began her prepared statement. "I've decided to seek a divorce. The children and I should not be subjected to the possibility of losing our financial security because you made an error in judgment in the operating room. I have a lawyer. We think you should obtain legal representation and settle quickly, before your malpractice case goes to trial. You should see to your wife and children's security while you still have the means."

Jack took a good look at Kate. She'd lost a fair amount of weight, had probably started working out again. He wondered if she'd already chosen her next victim. She always worked fast. Jack couldn't work any surprise into his voice. "My, you've been busy. What about the kids?"

"What about the kids? You've always spent more time pursuing your career than you've ever spent with them. They are well aware of your deficiencies. The children and I are hopeful you'll fulfill your responsibilities and support them in an appropriate manner."

Jack kept his voice neutral. "I want to speak with the kids right now."

"The children don't wish to talk to you. When visiting privileges and temporary child support are settled, I'll allow you to see them. You'll be too busy to see them in the near future anyway. You need to find a place to stay, and you need a lawyer."

A smile crept across Jack's face. "Tell me, are you going to reenter the work force? After all, you'll soon be a single mother."

"How could you or anyone else expect me to go back to work? This is a very stressful and emotional time for me. I have to face so many changes."

"It's tragic your dreams didn't work out."

"Get out!" Kate screamed. "Get out, you son of a bitch. I'm going to take you apart. I'm going to fuck you up. The kids and I depended on you, and you just couldn't make it. You're not tough, you're not strong. You'll lose that suit because you're weak. And then where will I be? You've ruined my life. I'll get my money before you manage to lose it."

"You know, Kate, this is the first genuine emotion I've seen from you in years."

Kate slammed the door in Jack's face.

Jack opened the garage door and backed out. He drove to a hotel that rented rooms by the week.

He couldn't miss work the next day. He had to generate money to pay lawyer fees. And it would take lots of money to rid himself of the woman he hated.

As he fell asleep, Jack realized the joke was on him.

CHAPTER TWENTY-ONE

Early the next morning Jack visited the local K-Mart and obtained enough basic clothing and toiletries to sustain him until he got a chance to reenter his former home to claim his possessions.

Before entering the OR locker room, Jack stopped at the charge nurse's desk. He asked her to make a note that all messages for him were to be routed to his cell phone only. No one should try to contact him at his old home phone number. He didn't offer any explanation, but figured his divorce proceedings would be common knowledge in the OR within thirty minutes.

He changed into his scrub clothes quickly, not wanting to encounter anyone in the locker room. Personal questions were more awkward to ask in the operating room environment, and he wished to avoid discussing anything of a private nature. Jack didn't want empathy. Empathy came at the price of revealing one's soul. It wasn't a fair trade. From this moment on, Jack's soul, if he had one, was his alone.

Jack went about his day's work, responding politely but without elaboration, to questions. At 11:45 a.m., Anne Taylor, a nurse known for aggressive gossip, came into Jack's room. She addressed him loudly. "Dr. Andrews, I see you no longer want anyone to use your home phone number. What does this mean?"

"It means my cell phone number is the one the OR should call if they want to deliver a message to me."

"Doctor, we'd all like to know what this change signifies."

"It doesn't signify anything for you or your nosy friends. If you have no questions concerning patient care, I suggest you mind your own business."

Case followed case and day followed day. Jack was excessively polite to people he didn't respect—his way of expressing disdain for them. He found he didn't have to be pleasant so long as he acted with formality and avoided outright sarcasm. Jack's patients found him cold and aloof, but could accept this because he exuded professionalism. The nurses and ancillary personnel in the OR were puzzled, then alarmed, at Jack's determination to avoid personal statements of any kind. He neither spoke of his own feelings nor was at all concerned with theirs. He never raised his voice in the OR. The effect was to reinforce the impression it would be foolish to tempt Dr. Andrews to genuine anger.

Jack's fellow physicians began having difficulty with him. Jack did what he thought best for every patient. He didn't compromise his care plan when a surgeon advocated another course of action. He not only wouldn't engage in debate, he didn't fake interest in any surgeon's opinion.

This resulted in Jack's caseload shrinking. Only the paucity of competent anesthesiologists stopped Jack's referrals from dropping to zero. Jack's indifference to his shrinking income was inexplicable to his fellow physicians. This behavior was unheard of in the private practice of medicine. Medicine is a business in the United States, and money is how the businessperson-physician keeps score.

The explanation favored by Jack's colleagues was that as soon as his malpractice suit was settled he'd overcome his aberrant mental state and once again play by the rules.

CHAPTER TWENTY-TWO

Three days after Kate's declaration Jack contacted a local law firm and inquired about obtaining another attorney, this one for divorce. When the receptionist discovered Jack Andrews's first name was Doctor she immediately connected him to one of the firm's senior partners.

The partner, Jordan Davis, made an attempt to express sympathy for poor Dr. Andrews, who now found himself in a sad situation, surely not his fault alone. Her audition to become his legal representative began. She tried, without success, to keep the rising enthusiasm out of her voice. "You know, Doctor, this case will have significant financial ramifications for you. A professional with your standing in the community is a tempting target for an angry ex-wife and her lawyer. They'll go after your existing assets and insist on high child support. You must have someone tough guarding your interests in the initial trial. After the marital assets are distributed there will be motions for increasing child support at regular intervals until the children are of age. This will go on for years."

"I'm aware of that," Jack mumbled.

"You have enormous professional responsibilities in the operating room. I can adjust my schedule so we can meet late in the afternoons or in the evenings after you complete your day's work."

"OK, Ms. Davis. Please have your secretary call me tomorrow so we can set up the initial appointment." Jack had to stifle a laugh as he hung up. He knew she wanted him busy so he could write her large checks over a long period of time.

CHAPTER TWENTY-THREE

A week later, Jack called his new malpractice attorney. "Hello, Flanders, Olsen, and Olsen," answered a receptionist in a bright, sunny voice.

"This is Dr. Jack Andrews. Mr. Jon Olsen has been retained to represent me in a legal action." Jack couldn't bring himself to say *malpractice case*. "May I speak with Mr. Olsen, please?"

The receptionist replied professionally, "I'll see if Mr. Olsen is in, sir." Jack waited to get an indication of how important his case was to Jon Olsen. Relative importance would be indicated by how long he was left on hold and whether it was Olsen or a subordinate who picked up.

Three minutes later the music from the local classical music station ended abruptly. "Hello, Dr. Andrews. This is Jon Olsen. I've been in contact with Peggy Jackson about your case. I'm looking forward to meeting you."

Jack thought Olsen's reply was pretty well done. A three-minute wait demonstrated Jon Olsen was a busy man, too busy to be instantly available. But the fact he personally answered the call meant no matter how busy he was, Dr. Jack Andrews was important to him. "Mr. Olsen, I'm pleased to speak with you. I'm aware of your contact with Ms. Jackson. She probably told you I lost confidence in the attorney she originally consulted."

"Well, umm, Ms. Jackson did mention that to me. Tell me, what was the disagreement between you and Ben Harris?"

"Harris wasn't interested in my case. He went into my deposition unprepared. The whole drill was just another payday for him. It was the first of many paydays he intended to gain at my expense."

"Dr. Andrews, the expense is paid by your insurer, not you."

Jack's voice smoldered into the phone. "The money involved in the legal process isn't what I'm talking about. The expense for me is the denigration of my professional reputation. I've spent my lifetime in education, training, and practicing medicine. I've got nothing in the world other than my professional competence and integrity. I cannot recover those things if they're taken away. This matter is not just a legal game to me."

"I assure you I will be absolutely serious about protecting your interests. What is it you want from me?"

Jack's voice went cold. "You can get me justice."

"Doctor, there are no guarantees in the legal arena. You know that."

Jack sounded as if he were incapable of emotion. "Don't worry, Mr. Olsen. I'll just ask you for your best effort. But I will have justice."

"Doctor, I have to fulfill another obligation at this time. May I transfer you to my secretary? She'll set up an appointment for you."

"Sure."

Jon Olsen, attorney-at-law, transferred the call. Then he sat back in his plush leather chair. He didn't know if he should be angry or scared or confused. Justice? Jon Olsen hadn't considered justice for some time.

CHAPTER TWENTY-FOUR

Jack's initial appointment with Jordan Davis took place on a Saturday morning ten days after he first contacted her office. Ms. Davis didn't mind working during the weekend. She smiled every time she envisioned the inevitably high legal fees this divorce case would generate. Having a doctor working for her during the next several years was so amusing.

Ms. Davis's paralegal, Susan McCalley, met Jack at the office door. She was a fortyish semi-attractive woman, impeccably dressed. She murmured something concerning sympathy for the soon-to-be-divorced doctor and led him to Ms. Davis's office. She promised to bring Jack a Diet Coke right away. Was there anything else he required? There wasn't, so Jack walked through the open door into the office as Susan hurried back down the corridor.

Ms. Davis rose from her seat and walked around a heavy, obviously expensive oak desk to shake Jack's hand. She looked to be in her late thirties with short blond hair and blue eyes, was attired in a fashionable pantsuit, and held wire-rimmed reading glasses in her left hand. She smiled in an ineffective attempt to exude warmth.

"Dr. Andrews, I'm glad to meet you. I wish it could have been under better circumstances."

Jack, amused in a fashion impossible for him only a few months earlier, said, "Are there any good circumstances in which a client hires a lawyer?"

"Good point, Doctor. Dealing with people who can't agree with each other is part and parcel of the legal profession."

"Counselor, let's get right to the point. My wife and I are going to be divorced. We've got two daughters. I don't want a messy trial. I just want this thing settled."

"Doctor, there's no such thing as an amicable divorce, particularly when there's money at stake. You can kid yourself all you want, but I assure you our opponents see you as a sheep to be sheared. If you believe there's some painless way out of your marriage, you're mistaken."

"Counselor, doesn't the law say all marital assets are divided in half? Why can't we just do that? I'll then agree to support the children. There must be some formula for that responsibility."

"Doctor, you have greater earning potential than your wife. She'll probably ask for a seventy-thirty split of your joint assets, and she'll probably be awarded fifty-five or sixty percent. As for child support, remember these are the children of a doctor. They can reasonably expect to continue to live the life to which they are accustomed. This will include lessons for whatever talent they possess, or think they possess, as well as trips, vacations, and a car when they reach sixteen. You're the source of all that. Your position entitles them to that."

"Tell me, Ms. Davis, what do these children deserve if their father decides to quit medicine? What happens if I decide I don't like being a doctor? Does their lifestyle sink to a lower level?"

"Let's get serious, Doctor. You're not going to quit medicine. No one's willing to cut his own income. If you try some stunt that results in a pay cut, the court will look at it as a voluntary choice. Then the court will probably force you to exhaust your share of the marital assets to keep the children's lifestyle appropriate for the children of a doctor."

"Much better to be related to a doctor than be a doctor yourself."

"Dr. Andrews, you've been rewarded by a society that allows you to occupy a position enabling you to generate a high income. Responsibilities come with that."

"It seems to me that society demanded I compete for selection into medical school, and then demanded I pass test after test over years of intense education and effort. And if I happen to be around when some member of that society encounters a bad result, society takes me apart. No questions asked."

"Quit being melodramatic, Doctor. You chose your life. You chose your wife. You chose divorce. I'll get you the best deal I can. This isn't about justice. It's about buying your way out of a situation. It's about money."

The conversation turned to practical matters. Matters like financial reports, temporary support of the wife and children, contact with Kate's attorney. All this would begin, of course, right after Dr. Andrews paid Ms. Davis an initial retainer of five thousand dollars. Did the doctor understand all this? He understood perfectly.

As she watched the doctor exit her office, Jordan Davis found herself in a terrific mood. She'd lead this doctor through the legal system by the nose. She and the opposing attorney would take turns discovering controversies. The answers to those controversies would require long hours of expensive legal research. The attorneys, along with their teams of accountants and paralegals, were going to do very well.

CHAPTER TWENTY-FIVE

Jack's days didn't change. He performed his work with mind-numbing competence. He had little heart for anesthesia, but discovered this made no difference to anyone but himself. He was a cog in the machine.

Occasionally Jack received a call from one of his two lawyers. Each was proceeding down a predictable legal path.

Ms. Davis and Kate's lawyer settled a deal for temporary support for Kate and the children. Kate's proposed budget was staggering, as expected. The lawyers arranged visitation for Jack with his daughters, but he found the girls generally had activities or parties at friends' houses during his appointed time. When he pulled them away from their plans they became sullen and uncommunicative. Jennifer and Sarah would, however, get in touch whenever they needed a little extra money. They believed these requests let Jack know they still considered him their father.

Ms. Davis's bills, delivered monthly, were mounting. Jack hoped the rest of her legal office operated as efficiently as her billing apparatus.

Jon Olsen handled the malpractice case with no input from Jack. Jack received updates as the legal process wound its ponderous way through the system. Olsen retained experts to defend Jack, the hospital retained experts to defend itself, and Carl Hafen retained experts to refute everything the defense experts declared.

The attorneys seemed only marginally interested in establishing exactly what had happened. They were more intent on producing a story the jury would buy. All that counted was a presentation to a group of twelve people carefully selected to exclude anyone with scientific education or advanced degrees of any kind. It was not unlike picking some fans from the stands of the Super Bowl and asking them to offici-ate the game.

Jack considered his present situation. His two opponents were intent on seizing his wealth and his future earnings. In addition, Hafen was anxious to ruin his professional reputation and thus make it impossible for him to recover. There was a lot of talent arrayed against him and he had no chance to prevail.

He adjusted to the new reality.

Jack decided once these lawsuits were complete he'd never again expose himself to the vagaries of civil law in the United States. He stayed in the hotel, paying rent one month in advance. He acquired no furniture, no savings account, no new friends. He never contributed to his retirement fund. When his two legal hells were over he'd never be tempted to return to the life he had so long ago, and so mistakenly, aspired to lead.

CHAPTER TWENTY-SIX

Eight months later, Kate called Jack and got right to the point. "I want this divorce settled as soon as possible. It's not fair for the children and me to have to wait while your lawyer drags everything out. We can't begin a new life with this divorce hanging over us."

"Gee, Kate, that surprises me. Knowing you as well as I do, I would've bet you'd delay the process as long as possible. You think I'm weak, so you'd wager I'd get crushed emotionally by two lawsuits. Then I couldn't resist even the bad deal you and your lawyer offered."

"Listen, you bastard, your choices are either give me the money or give it to the dead guy's lawyer."

"Well said. I see why you like this approach. It's always best to be the first predator to feed on the prey."

"If you don't close the deal soon, Jack, I'll make sure the girls have nothing to do with you again. Ever." The line went dead.

Jack decided to leave one of his nightmares behind. He directed Jordan Davis to buy his freedom from Kate. So, on a fine, sunny day, all the parties met in a courtroom for an arbitration session. Kate received 60 percent of the marital assets. Child support was set at a rate of roughly two times the usual level because Jennifer and Sarah were the children of a physician. Kate was even awarded something unusual in the age of feminism—three years' alimony. No one in the legal system could conceive of forcing her to make the difficult transition to living on a nurse's wage. Not for a while, anyway.

The total amount paid to lawyers during this legal adventure was one hundred thousand dollars.

Jordan Davis, attorney-at-law and the person most concerned with Dr. Jack Andrews's welfare, was disappointed. Had the case gone to trial she might have doubled the thirty-eight thousand dollars she'd personally earned so far. She did, however, have happy thoughts as she walked out of the courtroom, her client in tow. "That was pretty standard, Doctor. When one of the spouses has an ability to make a lot more money than the other the court often splits assets sixty-forty. Of course, you realize all child support agreements are subject to amendment. We'll probably be back in court in a couple of years to reevaluate everything."

"If everything was so standard, why did it require so much time and all those expensive experts?" Jack replied cynically. "Why didn't you two attorneys just settle?"

Jordan Davis didn't like this man. If he didn't have two young children and a resourceful ex-wife who'd demand several visits back to court in the next eight or nine years, she'd cut him loose. "Doctor, we had to make sure no one cheated on determining your net worth and your potential for future earnings. And the court demands the children's budget be carefully evaluated. The court is very mindful of the children's welfare."

"Counselor, everyone knows exactly how concerned the opposing attorneys were with the children's welfare. Neither of you spared any legal expense in your effort to gain the standard result."

Davis couldn't release this cash cow. "Go home and reflect on the case. You had no choice but to buy your way out of this marriage, and you did it. Be glad it's over."

Jack smiled with his mouth, not his eyes. "Oh, I'm glad. And you should be glad too. Your future in the business of legal coercion is getting brighter and brighter."

CHAPTER TWENTY-SEVEN

Three months after the divorce Jon Olsen called Jack. "Doctor, the trial date for your case has been set. It'll occur eighteen months from now. A year from next November. Mr. Hafen persuaded the court he'd require a four-week trial to present a case with so many complex and compelling factors. The court is overwhelmed with civil cases and therefore a four-week block must be scheduled far in advance."

Jack grunted.

"So," Olsen said in a voice indicating Jack had no choice but to cooperate, "is there any problem, Doctor?"

"Counselor, the trial date is over three years after the event. That's a long time for me to wait. Aren't there rules mandating a speedy resolution of legal cases?"

Olsen, impatient, replied, "Doctor, this isn't a criminal trial. It's a civil complaint. It's about money. You shouldn't let it weigh on you. Just go on with your life. Of course there will be ongoing legal maneuvers, most of them taking place the last two or three months before the trial. Who knows, we may be able to settle this case. Probably, we will. You should just relax while your defense team works everything out."

"Mr. Olsen, this case isn't going to be settled. I didn't do anything wrong and I want my day in court. I want to win. Are you with me?"

"Doctor, over the next eighteen months you might change your mind. You may decide to get this monkey off your back. I say again, this is only about money. Nothing personal is involved." Olsen paused, then added with emphasis, "And anyway, the malpractice company is in charge of the defense. If they decide it's in their best interest to settle, they'll settle. If that's the decision they make they won't feel it necessary to gain your permission."

"I see. The legal system puts the trial far into the future. They believe they can wear me down over time, make me compliant. The insurance company cares about its bottom line, and all the attorneys make a ton of money. The only thing to suffer is my professional reputation, right?"

"Doctor, this will be a whole lot easier on everyone if you lay your pride and emotions aside."

"I don't want this thing to be a whole lot easier for everyone." Jack hung up and began to get himself ready.

CHAPTER TWENTY-EIGHT

Jack spent the next year fighting a growing sense of hopelessness, reminding himself daily that only his immediate future lay in the hands of his enemies. He would determine his ultimate fate.

He decided two things were of supreme importance for him. First, he'd have justice, something he could achieve only by himself. No committee, no court, no counselors would be permitted to determine what constituted justice. Second, he'd never again lead a life limited by a desire to accumulate personal wealth. That was how his society kept score. He and society were going to part ways.

Jack continued living in the hotel, not wanting a permanent home or anything else that might impede him when he decided to leave. He ate irregularly, only when he became genuinely hungry. He lost weight, discovering anger and outrage were more effective than self-discipline for achieving weight loss.

Anger was his friend. Self-pity was for the weak.

He worked out obsessively every day, absolutely certain a high level of conditioning was essential for seizing his fate. His body weight dropped to a rock-hard one hundred seventy pounds, the same weight he'd carried twenty years before as a small college wide receiver.

The big game was coming. He needed an edge. Preparation was the key.

He found peace at a local indoor pistol range, shooting an hour at a time, precision his only goal. During that hour nothing touched him, nothing mattered except the front sight. Execution of a precise shot meant Jack had, for a moment, not allowed the world to interfere with him. Concentration became his drug.

Jack had studied Taoism in a required religion course before starting medical school. Three of its tenets were: Detachment. Forgetfulness of results. Abandonment of hope for reward.

He found those words profound.

CHAPTER TWENTY-NINE

Jack's hermit-like existence drew attention from his coworkers. One day a very good-looking nurse positioned herself in his path as he walked down the OR corridor. Her name was Sally Vogel, and she was well known for her perfect body, her exquisite taste in clothes, and her ability to be exceptionally friendly with men of adequate financial resources. Three years divorced from her stockbroker husband, she was always eager to enlarge her circle of friends. "Dr. Andrews," she purred, "nobody's seen you on the social circuit. We're all wondering when you'll get back into the swing of things. If you stay in this all-work-and-no-play routine, you'll become a dull boy."

Jack didn't care for Sally Vogel. She reminded him of Kate. He said, "You know, Sally, the truth is, I'm gay. I'm thinking of coming out of the closet."

"Oh, really, Doctor, we all know better than that. If you don't find someone soon, I'll have to seduce you myself."

Jack's stomach turned. "Sally, in the unlikely event I ever need another woman, I'll hire a pro. She'd cost much less than you in the long run and she'd be more honest."

Sally Vogel, face red, turned on her heel and stomped away. Jack watched her go and smiled genuinely for the first time in many days. No one in the operating room felt compelled to inquire about Jack's social life again.

Jack tried only once to spend an entire weekend with his daughters. He took them to lunch and then to a movie.

As they left the theater, Jennifer stated, "Dad, now that the movie's over you have to take us back to our house right away."

"Oh, I thought I'd take you out to a nice dinner. After dinner, we can go back to where I live and you can tell me about your schoolwork and activities. Then I'll take you home. Tomorrow we can go out to a nice brunch and later visit the zoo."

Jennifer, with sarcasm learned at Kate's knee, said, "You can quit being a Disneyland dad. I have plans to go to a party at my friend's house. The whole class will be there. Mom says, since I'm going out, Sarah can have two friends over for a slumber party. It's past five now and we have to be home by six. Just take us home. Now."

Sarah piped up, "Yes, Dad, my friends are coming over at six. We're going to watch movies and make popcorn and play."

Jack, taken aback, said, "How could you make plans for the one weekend a month you're supposed to be with me?"

Jennifer impatiently straightened her father out. "Dad, if you were really interested in being a good father you wouldn't have left Mom in such a poor financial situation. Mom even said so. Mom says it's your responsibility to support us and you haven't done a very good job. You have no right to tell us what to do. We want to see our friends tonight. Now can we please go home?"

Sarah became very quiet. So did Jack. He walked to his car, the girls trailing behind. He unlocked the doors. Everyone put a seat belt on. He drove straight back to his old house. Jennifer walked directly to the house, opened the door, and went in. Sarah stopped at the entrance, turned, and made a little wave to Jack. He waved back. The door closed.

From then on Saturday visits with the girls became infrequent. One or the other of the girls usually had an activity at school or a pressing social engagement. They could barely spare more than a few minutes when Jack called them.

As time passed, Jack began dreading calls initiated by either of his daughters. Every contact was a request for money. He always forked over the money in the hope things might get better. That is, he did until Jennifer informed him it was his responsibility to give her two thousand dollars for a ten-day camp at a horse ranch. She stated he owed her the money because he didn't do anything else for her. After that call he paid precisely the amount the court ordered for child support and quit calling his daughters. Occasionally, he envisioned a day when they'd regard him as a father, not just a banker. In his darker moments he realized the absurdity of such thoughts.

And so he went through the motions. He collected his pay and paid his bills. He fulfilled his responsibilities. He existed. Then one day Jon Olsen called him. The trial would begin in three months.

Time for the end game.

CHAPTER THIRTY

Preparation for the trial began in earnest. Jon Olsen and his staff familiarized themselves with every fact and opinion in the thousands of pages of documents the lawsuit had generated. The legal team pored over depositions given by the opponent's expert witnesses.

They also studied the numerous depositions those same experts had offered in other medical malpractice lawsuits across the country. Testifying for plaintiffs' attorneys is a lucrative business. The medical-legal luminaries in this cadre are not chosen for their knowledge, professional standing, or expertise. They are chosen because they appear distinguished and will say whatever the attorney wants them to say.

Defense attorneys like Jon Olsen don't have the medical background necessary to determine the truth of expert testimony. Nor are they concerned with the truth. What Olsen wanted to find was any inconsistency in opinions offered during previous testimony, inconsistencies he could use to destroy the experts' credibility. No one thought any jury remotely recognized medical truth or medical uncertainties. The trick was to make the jury trust your experts more than those of your opponent.

Jack spent several hours each Saturday at his lawyer's office learning the art of testifying before a jury. He was instructed to speak to the jury in the same way he spoke with patients before an operation. He was not to raise his voice or display anger under any circumstance. He was not to act defensively. Dr. Jack Andrews must personify the practicing physician who possessed the common sense and medical knowledge necessary to care for patients.

To ensure he reacted properly in court, Olsen and his associates put him through long and hostile questioning sessions. They critiqued each performance. The legal people always pointed out they weren't trying to influence his opinions. It would be unethical for them to coach the doctor on his testimony. They were just trying to help him tell his story. The lawyers were meticulous in paying lip service to proper ethical conduct. Over and over they stated their job was to make sure the jury saw Dr. Andrews in the best possible light.

It became obvious they didn't trust Dr. Jack Andrews.

Jack entered the courthouse on the first day of his trial with a deep sense of shame because he was the defendant in a medical malpractice lawsuit. His eyes remained downcast—he dreaded meeting anyone he knew. He wasn't defiant. He sought only survival on the lawyers' turf. This was alien territory for him. His enemies were as aware of this as he, and they were sure to capitalize on it.

The first two days of the trial were devoted to jury selection. Carl Hafen was most attentive to this process. He had the right to question potential jurors thoroughly, and he ruthlessly disqualified people capable of independent thought. College graduates were unacceptable as jurors in this trial. Members of the military need not apply. Any professional who accepted personal responsibility for his or her decisions was dismissed.

However, people who reacted to questions with emotion rather than judgment were welcomed aboard.

Dr. Jack Andrews was definitely not going to be judged by a jury of his peers.

Opening statements began on the third day. Carl Hafen began his remarks by noting it was his duty to bring a tragic case before this jury—a case in which Dr. Jack Andrews had undoubtedly caused the untimely death of Mr. Robert Parker, the husband of his client. Mrs. Parker was the mother of a young child for whom she was now solely responsible. Hafen admitted the deceased and his client had not lived together for a year before Bob's death, but the jury knew all relationships encountered a few rough spots, and this relationship would surely have healed, if only the husband and wife had not been robbed of the precious time necessary to reconcile.

Then Hafen made his most important point. "Ladies and gentlemen of the jury, I must remind you of the judge's instructions. This is not a criminal trial where guilt must be proved beyond a reasonable doubt. This is a civil trial where the legal standard states you must decide on the preponderance of the evidence. What that means is this: If you believe my interpretation of what caused Mr. Parker's death is even slightly more plausible than Dr. Andrews's version of events, even one percent more likely, then you must find for the plaintiff. It's the way the American system of justice works, and justice is what we all want." Hafen sat down to comfort his tearful client.

Enlightenment rushed to Jack Andrews. He understood. This lawyer didn't have to prove his allegations. He was licensed to twist and misrepresent facts. All he had to do was create a small amount of doubt in a small group of laypeople. The jurors were empowered to judge events despite their complete medical ignorance. The legal game was all about creating uncertainty. Truth didn't matter.

Jack tried to hide his cynicism and despair.

The first witness for the plaintiff was Dr. Charles Kessler. He was the chairman of a small anesthesia department that served an inner city hospital in Chicago. The hospital maintained an affiliation with the University of Illinois. This university affiliation conferred to him a certain amount of academic respectability. Dr. Kessler, in his early sixties, was a small, thin, bald man. His never-exercised body was soft, pallid, and wrinkled. A perpetual frown emanated from a remarkably homely face. His colleagues believed this unpleasant appearance reflected a nasty, bitter disposition. He believed he deserved to head a world-renowned academic anesthesia program. This was never going to happen. He attributed this failure to establishment academic snobbery that failed to recognize the inherent worth of his innovative approach to the science of anesthesiology. In reality the problem stemmed from the quality of his research, which was neither original nor important.

His second overwhelming characteristic was greed. It took a lot of money to live the way he felt he deserved to live. He'd discovered a way to supplement his relatively meager academic income. Dr. Kessler advertised in legal journals, touting his ability to build effective malpractice cases against his fellow physicians. He noted the enormous number of such cases in which he'd participated. He inflated his academic credentials. Nowhere did he express interest in the merits of a case. He became a success. A long list of attorneys retained him. They admired his lack of ethics and his ability to lie. He had long ago become a regular on Team Hafen.

Carl Hafen stood in front of his star witness. "Dr. Kessler, have you reviewed the case in question? The anesthesia that resulted in the death of Bob Parker?"

Dr. Kessler replied in a strong voice, demonstrating he had no doubts concerning the facts. "Yes, I have fully reviewed the entire medical record. I have further reviewed the depositions of everyone involved. I am familiar with all the facts of this case."

In a voice hinting at regret for being forced to reveal difficult matters, Hafen asked, "What conclusions have you reached, Doctor?"

Charles Kessler made eye contact with the jury. "I am convinced this patient received an overdose of morphine in the recovery room. This overdose of the narcotic morphine slowed the patient's respiration to the point where he became hypoxic. That is, the amount of oxygen contained in his blood dropped because he was breathing inadequately. This inadequate oxygenation caused damage to the alveoli, which are the microscopic areas of the lung where the exchange of oxygen for carbon dioxide takes place. These alveoli are really just very small sacs. The damage from the lack of oxygen caused a breakdown of the cells that line these sacs, allowing fluid from the bloodstream to leak in. Of course, once those sacs, the alveoli, filled with fluid, they could no longer take part in the exchange of oxygen into the blood. The patient's oxygenation continued to worsen and a vicious cycle began. As the patient was denied more and more oxygen, more and more sacs filled with fluid. The patient inevitably died."

Hafen paused for dramatic effect, then intoned, "Doctor, are you positive Mr. Parker died from an overdose of the narcotic morphine?"

Kessler looked at each juror in turn before saying, with a twinge of sympathy in his voice, "I believe it is beyond a reasonable degree of medical certainty that this is what caused Mr. Parker's death."

Hafen asked, "Why do you suppose Dr. Jack Andrews prescribed such a large dose of morphine in the recovery room? An overdose large enough to kill Bob Parker?"

Kessler had no doubts. "I believe Dr. Andrews probably just wanted Bob Parker to be quiet. Dr. Andrews wanted to start his next case, a craniotomy, and Bob was complaining of post-operative pain, that is, pain due to his stomach operation. Dr. Andrews couldn't begin his next case until his previous patient stopped complaining of pain."

Hafen, outraged, said, "You mean Dr. Andrews negligently administered an overdose of the narcotic morphine to Bob Parker just so he could make a few hundred dollars for performing anesthesia on a craniotomy patient? Wouldn't that be murder?"

Dr. Kessler assumed the facial expression of someone familiar with the evil in this world. "I'd class it more as an accidental death. Like manslaughter. Dr. Andrews didn't intend to kill Mr. Parker. He just didn't care."

"Dr. Kessler, how much money does an anesthesiologist like Dr. Andrews make for performing an anesthetic for a craniotomy?"

"Probably eight hundred to twelve hundred dollars."

"But, Dr. Kessler, even though that's a lot of money, is it really enough to tempt a physician to be negligent?"

"I'm afraid the facts speak for themselves."

With righteous indignation Hafen said, "The defense is going to claim that none of what you describe is true. They're going to claim the patient died of an allergic reaction. Is there any possibility that an allergic reaction could have caused Bob Parker's death?"

"Absolutely not. Mr. Parker had been previously exposed to every drug he was given on the day in question. He never reacted to those drugs before, and there's no reason to believe he reacted to any of them on the day he died."

"Dr. Kessler, could Mr. Parker have reacted to any of the blood transfusions he received? Could he have had an allergic reaction to the blood itself?"

"There is no possibility this patient's death was caused by a blood transfusion. The blood transfusion was completed in the operating room. If the blood transfusion caused Mr. Parker's death he would have shown obvious signs of distress while still in the operating room. We all know he encountered problems only after he was in the recovery room a considerable length of time. It is ludicrous to even suggest the blood transfusion as a possible cause of death."

"Dr. Kessler, was the physician's response—that is, was Dr. Andrews's response—within the standard of care in regard to the hypoxia Mr. Parker suffered from the morphine overdose?"

"Absolutely not. Dr. Andrews didn't recognize the problem soon enough. He belatedly called in experts who performed heroically in an effort to save Mr. Parker's life, but they could do nothing. They weren't called in time. The overdose of the narcotic morphine, coupled with Dr. Andrews's inattention to this patient's immediate problems, doomed Mr. Parker. If Dr. Andrews had not been so intent on beginning the next case, Bob Parker would still be alive."

Carl Hafen, speaking with regret in his voice, said, "Thank you, Dr. Kessler. It's a sad story, but one that must be brought out."

The judge called a recess. Jack and Jon Olsen walked to a private meeting area down the hall from the courtroom. Jon Olsen was serious. "That was compelling testimony. Dr. Kessler is going to cause us trouble."

Jack said, "What he testified is completely untrue. The patient was not overdosed with narcotics. He was talking until he was reintubated. If he suffered such severe oxygen deprivation that the cells in his lungs were breaking down, he wouldn't have been able to talk. In fact, that amount of oxygen deprivation would have already killed his brain cells. He would have been comatose. This whole fantasy of Dr. Kessler is a medical impossibility. I had to put him to sleep with propofol before I could replace the breathing tube, for fuck's sake. Anyone who knows anything about medicine and thinks just a little about what happened knows the story Kessler just told is a complete fabrication. You've got to bring the truth out."

Olsen looked across the table at his client. "Doctor, the truth really doesn't matter. It's how the story plays with the jury. They were eating that testimony up. If I get too rough with the good Dr. Kessler, they'll be angry with me. And you. I have to go in there and see if I can create some doubt about Kessler's credibility."

Olsen's cross-examination was formal, almost polite. The doctor stuck with his story. He maintained his interpretation of the facts were correct to a reasonable degree of medical certainty.

Olsen asked, "Dr. Kessler, you maintain this patient died because of a hypoxic event. You maintain hypoxia—that is a relative decrease in the oxygen carried by the blood—caused a breakdown of the alveoli and thus a release of fluid into the lungs. This fluid in the lungs doomed the patient. How could such a degree of hypoxia be present in view of the fact the patient's oxygen saturation was always maintained above eighty-five percent? And how could Bob Parker have talked to Dr. Andrews if he were so hypoxic? Isn't it true the brain cells are the body part most sensitive to hypoxia—that is, lack of oxygen?"

Kessler smiled condescendingly at Jon Olsen. "First, in my opinion, the alveoli are much more sensitive to hypoxia than brain cells. Second, I'm not certain the patient's oxygen saturation or his mental status were really good. We have only the word of Dr. Andrews and his nurses to that. It's to their advantage to stick to that story. I noticed Dr. Andrews intubated Mr. Parker before anyone else could examine him. This, of course, precludes a neurologic exam by another physician. I believe Dr. Andrews and his minions knew they'd made a mistake and started a cover-up immediately."

The jury members sat on the edges of their seats. They'd all heard stories of cover-ups by people occupying positions of trust. They'd been conditioned by the news media to believe that authority figures abused their power and then lied about what really happened. Dr. Kessler's last statement resonated with them. It fed directly into their basic distrust of the system.

In a final attempt to undermine the witness, Olsen queried, "Dr. Kessler, how much money did you charge the plaintiff's attorney to testify today?"

Dr. Kessler, not embarrassed, said, "I received nine thousand dollars."

"Isn't that an enormous amount of money for your services?"

"I've spent hours studying the record, trying to find something that could persuade me that the conclusions I reached were not true. Those hours were spent in vain. The sad fact is my conclusions are correct. A thorough investigation to find the truth is time-consuming and expensive. But the truth, counselor, is worth uncovering."

Olsen had no more questions. The court recessed for lunch.

The first witness called in the afternoon session was Dr. Jack Andrews. Hafen asked his first question. "Dr. Andrews, isn't it true the actions you took in the recovery room, while caring for Bob Parker, led directly to his death?"

Jon Olsen objected. The judge had the question stricken from the record and told the jurors to disregard it. The jurors never forgot the moment or the question.

Hafen proceeded to question Jack with confidence and purpose. "Dr. Andrews, were you the physician who administered the general anesthetic to Robert Parker on the day he died?"

With visible effort, Jack raised his gaze from the floor to make eye contact with Hafen. Regretfully he said, "I was."

"Then you were also the physician responsible for Mr. Parker's care in the recovery room, weren't you?"

As instructed, Jack shifted his head position to look directly at the jury. The movement looked forced. The jury members stared back at him with wide, unblinking eyes. "Yes."

"Doctor, why do you think Bob Parker died under your care?"

"He must have died from an allergic reaction."

"Really, Doctor? You claim he must have died from an allergic reaction? Then, Doctor, he must have died from a reaction to a specific drug or a specific substance he was exposed to. Allergic reactions don't just fall out of the sky. You must agree there had to be a culprit."

Jack fidgeted and leaned backward just a little in the witness chair. "That's correct, but I don't know what it was. No one knows. Most likely it was some unknown substance in one of the units of blood I had to administer. The patient's reaction just overwhelmed him."

"The patient? You refer to him as just the patient?" Hafen's voice was condescending. "The person involved had a name. His name was Robert Parker and he's dead."

"I meant no disrespect."

"Of course not, Doctor." Hafen, shocked at Jack's failure to recognize Bob Parker's humanity, shook his head and went on. "You heard Dr. Kessler. How do you answer his testimony that an allergic reaction to something administered in the operating room would have declared itself immediately?"

"Allergic reactions are unpredictable."

"Your response to that statement is more predictable than an allergic reaction, isn't that right, Doctor?"

A juror nodded his head.

Hafen renewed his attack. "You disagree with Dr. Kessler?"

"Yes—"

Hafen cut Jack off. "You think you're smarter than Dr. Kessler, don't you? In fact, you think you're smarter than just about everyone. That's why you bullied Dr. Kim Stevens and Dr. Larry Walker and forced them to abandon the usual therapy for Bob Parker's condition. You actually insisted on using cardiopulmonary bypass for what you say was an allergic reaction. An allergic reaction! The treatment they prescribed wasn't radical enough for you, was it? You did something that's never been tried in the history of medicine. You experimented on Bob Parker, didn't you?"

Jon Olsen objected. Carl Hafen promised to observe courtroom decorum. The jury watched in rapt attention.

Hafen, now in complete control, asked, "Doctor Andrews, why did you take control of the patient away from Drs. Walker and Stevens?"

Jack's voice rose in pitch and words tumbled out too rapidly. "Their therapy wasn't working. It would never have worked. The patient... Robert Parker...was going to arrest. Something had to be done."

"Something had to be done because, in fact, Doctor, you had placed Robert Parker in an impossible situation, a situation no other physician could reverse."

"Nothing was working. He was dying." Jack looked at his feet. His voice became almost inaudible. "I had to do the right thing."

"I also have to do the right thing, Doctor. Right now, that's determining who killed Bob Parker. Now, why didn't you call in your backup anesthesiologist, Dr. Adams, to perform anesthesia for the case that followed Mr. Parker's operation on the night in question?"

"Mr. Parker was stable. I proceeded with the next emergency case, just as we do every night on call."

"But Bob Parker wasn't stable, was he? In fact, he was deteriorating right in front of your eyes in the recovery room. Doctor, is the recovery room an intensive care unit, a unit where a patient is expected to require special observation?"

"Yes."

"So, instead of observing and recognizing a patient poised on the precipice, you prescribed Bob Parker the narcotic morphine to quiet him down. That way you could avoid listening to him complain of pain and wouldn't have to call in another anesthesiologist. And you'd make more money." Hafen paused, "Was the money worth it, Doctor?"

"There was no sign Mr. Parker wasn't recovering from anesthesia in a routine manner."

"Obviously a competent physician, a physician more interested in Bob Parker's fragile condition than you were, would have disagreed with you."

"Look, Mr. Parker was doing well. He wasn't having any trouble at the time we started the craniotomy."

"Oh, Doctor, I think you knew he was in trouble. That's why you intubated him before Dr. Adams reached the hospital. In fact, you left another patient unattended in the operating room to do just that. Another example of your inattention to a physician's duty."

"I had no choice."

Hafen thundered, "You had choices and you made decisions. You decided to abandon a patient on an operating room table while you rushed to the recovery room to intubate Bob Parker before Dr. Adams, Dr. Stevens, or Dr. Walker could examine him. You never gave them a chance to evaluate Mr. Parker's neurologic condition because they'd have discovered you'd left Mr. Parker severely impaired. Your cover-up was immediate."

"That's not what happened." Jack was catatonic.

"The facts speak for themselves, Doctor. They cry out for justice for Bob Parker."

Hafen had no other questions.

CHAPTER THIRTY-ONE

Jon Olsen began his cross-examination of Jack the following morning. He asked questions designed to illustrate how Jack had made each successive decision. Olsen wished to introduce the jurors to the uncertainty inherent in caring for a suddenly critically endangered patient. He wanted the jury to feel the gut-wrenching anguish that accompanied life-or-death situations.

Jon Olsen did his best, but he failed.

Jack looked into the faces of the jurors and faced reality. They didn't understand scientific arguments, and they had no way of determining which expert was correct. These people, however well-meaning, were conditioned by their society. They didn't trust authority figures, and they were indifferent to the difficulty of making critical decisions. They believed a doctor should always save the patient. That's why doctors made so much money.

What resonated with these jurors was a suspicion that doctors made mistakes. Lots of mistakes. And mistakes led to cover-ups.

They also believed some doctors ignored patients' best interests because the doctors wanted to perform more procedures and make more money.

Finally, the society inhabited by these jurors demanded no patient ever experience a bad result. If there was a bad result, someone in authority must be at fault. In this particular case, poor Bob Parker was dead. Dr. Jack Andrews was in charge and therefore must have contributed to the tragedy. Dr. Andrews was a rich doctor. He deserved to be disciplined. Justice demanded it.

The trial went on for two more weeks. Plaintiff experts challenged defense witnesses, and vice versa. The jurors became fatigued and bored. They wanted to make a decision. The lawyers concluded further arguments were useless and probably counter-productive. Neither of them could do anything more to influence the verdict. The judge sent the jurors out with specific instructions and told them to come back with a verdict.

Jon Olsen called two days later and told Jack to return to the courtroom. Jack had already accepted the inevitable result. The only question was the amount.

Jack stood as the jurors announced their decision. He was exhausted and his world dark.

The jury found Dr. Jack Andrews negligent and awarded the plaintiff $1.25 million.

Hafen, jubilant, hugged his client.

Jack found himself back in his hotel room two hours later. He didn't know how he'd gotten there.

CHAPTER THIRTY-TWO

The trial had been expected to last four weeks. Jack had taken a month's vacation and awoke the morning after the verdict with a week unscheduled. He took stock of his situation. His share of the marital assets totaled about $550,000. About half was in a retirement plan and the other half could be converted into cash.

He remembered how idealistic he'd been when he began medical school and marveled at his youthful naiveté. He'd believed success in medicine ensured respect, financial security, and a happy home life. He'd sacrificed much for that goal. Now, he was forty years old, burned out, and broke. His medical career was irreparably tarnished. He didn't have enough energy to recover.

He'd been a fool.

But every person, even Jack Andrews, deserved justice.

Jon Olsen called at ten o'clock in the morning. "Doctor, first let me say how shocked I was with the verdict. The jurors probably decided to give money to the family out of sympathy. They see you as a rich doctor and the patient's family as destitute. We will, of course, begin the appeal process."

Jack replied with an edge in his voice, "There aren't going to be any appeals. An appeals process takes months or even years. I can't change my life while that's going on. My malpractice policy is good for a million. I'll come up with the other quarter million myself. Find out where the money needs to be transferred so I can end the legal process. After the financial deal is complete I don't want to hear from the court or the plaintiff or Carl Hafen or you again. Call me back when you've made the arrangements."

An astounded Jon Olsen said, "Doctor, I've never heard of anyone wanting to end the litigation process by dipping into his own funds voluntarily. Everyone fights to get the plaintiff to accept a figure covered by the insurance company. I know you have the potential for making a lot of money, but paying two hundred and fifty thousand dollars has got to be a crippling financial blow for you."

"Mr. Olsen, I'm going to leave private practice as soon as I can. I won't delay my plans so a bunch of lawyers can argue. Do what I've asked."

Olsen planned to pursue prolonged legal maneuvers. As far as he was concerned the meter was still running. "Doctor, you're just saying that because of disappointment you're feeling at this moment. No one gives up a high-paying job. No one."

"Stay tuned."

CHAPTER THIRTY-THREE

Jack contacted his financial advisor. He had $202,000 in retirement accounts. The remainder of his wealth, $358,000, was in stocks and bonds. He instructed the advisor to sell everything not in the retirement program and deposit the cash into his checking account. The advisor attempted to dissuade him. The conversation ended quickly and sharply.

After he hung up, Jack considered his untouched retirement plan. A person never knew. He might actually live long enough to qualify for retirement.

At noon the phone rang. Dr. Richard Madison, calling in his capacity as chair of the quality assurance committee, greeted Jack. His was, as always, pretentious. "Dr. Andrews, I received word of the verdict this morning. In light of the fact you'll now be listed in the National Practitioner Data Bank as a physician who's lost a malpractice claim, it will be necessary to begin a review process. We'll be forced to reevaluate your anesthesia privileges. There isn't a rush to do this. Your privileges are good until the anniversary of their issuance. That will be approximately six months from now. I just wanted to let you know so you'll be prepared."

"You don't wait a minute to throw your weight around, do you? By the way, Richard, are you still specializing in hernia repairs and hysterectomies?"

"That's the attitude that's always caused you difficulty," Madison growled. "It will continue to cause trouble for you in the future."

"You're right, Richard, I should be more like you. I should spend my time telling other physicians what they should have done in tight situations, while always making damn sure I never personally get involved in a case requiring skill or judgment."

The phone registered a thump as the handset on the other end slammed into the receiver.

CHAPTER THIRTY-FOUR

Jack spent the next few days taking long walks, evaluating how he'd been exploited, exploited by a legal system he'd underestimated. Sure, Kate and Carl Hafen were actors in the drama, but they were inevitable products of the legal system. Just like he was.

He knew, if he were willing to work and struggle, he might recover financially over many years. But then he'd have to again become part of the unjust system.

The truth was buried, unintelligible. Many people had vested financial interests in twisting events. They hid truth in return for money. Did they know they would get away with their crimes? Sure.

They knew they'd get away because they believed they were immune to retribution. The law said retribution was illegal. Society said retribution was immoral. And the legal profession depended on the fact their victims were too weak to seek vengeance.

What was he going to do about that? Could he change society? No. Could he make legal professionals seek justice and truth? Ridiculous.

All Jack Andrews could do was leave this society, but before he did, he'd make a few exploiters pay.

He mustn't get caught. He was no martyr. What he wanted was payback. Society had used its rules against him. Those same rules ensured he could take his revenge and get away with it.

He considered timing and weather. He needed a way to get around the country anonymously and concluded a motorcyclist wearing a helmet with a dark visor left no facial signature. Also, motorcycle license plates were small and thus harder to read.

It was autumn now. He'd begin the necessary skills training in the spring. The plan must be completed before snow fell again. Motorcycles weren't effective means of transportation on snow-packed roads. Next March he'd trade his Land Rover for a motorcycle. The trade was necessary because by March he'd possess less than one hundred thousand dollars after paying off the malpractice ruling. His plan required access to cash. The car had to go.

From this moment on he'd pay every bill in cash. His activities would attract hunters, and hunters follow trails. At the very least he'd leave no money trail.

He required weapons. All firearms he currently possessed were easily traceable. They could serve only as a diversion. His weapon requirements were simple: they must be accurate, concealable, and untraceable. He needed two handguns and a rifle. The rifle must be capable of disassembly without loss of zero in its sight system. These instruments had to be obtained in a city distant from Omaha and purchased with cash.

He'd live and work quietly the next few months. The only goal he need accomplish over the winter was the theft of useful drugs from the hospital. When springtime arrived he'd initiate motorcycle skills and weapons training.

Finally, he'd perfect a means of escape.

Social debridement required precise planning.

He laughed to himself. His medical education had imprinted the need for preparation and contingency planning. He already enjoyed this new game.

CHAPTER THIRTY-FIVE

An idea awakened Jack at four o'clock. It was more a revelation. He showered and shaved. Now it was 4:45 a.m. He walked to an all-night diner, ate a farmhand's breakfast, drank two cups of coffee, and read the previous day's newspaper. Time moved slowly. He returned to his hotel room and waited.

Jack's friend from college, Fred Simons, lived in New York City. At eight, Jack called information. Information had a number for Simons's office, and, for an additional dollar, rang it.

A receptionist with the irritating nasal New York City accent picked up. "American Council for Missionary Services. May I help you?"

"This is Dr. Jack Andrews." His voice radiated professionalism. "I knew Reverend Fred Simons in college. I wonder if I might speak with him."

The receptionist, conditioned to speak with respect to anyone with the first name *Doctor*, said, "Yes, Dr. Andrews, if you'll hold, I'll see if Reverend Simons is available."

"Hello?" The voice sounded as if it belonged to an actor trained for the stage. "Is this the same Jack Andrews who repeatedly led me astray during my younger years?"

"It is, Fred. We did have some great times, didn't we? I saw an article about you in the alumni journal a couple of years ago. It was nice to see you'd moved back to the States and become director of your organization."

"You know, Jack, I spent about ten years abroad. Then I got pretty badly messed up in a car accident. The medical care at the mission allowed me to survive, barely, but I'm not mobile anymore, though

I'm thankful to be alive. Perhaps if I hadn't had to wait a week to get an evacuation flight out of my African village things might have healed better. Anyway, the church doesn't feel a handicapped person is the best choice for remote missionary work. They decided to make an administrator out of me. We all serve as best we can."

"I'm sorry, Fred. You were always a tough guy. Hardest hitting linebacker we had. I know nothing will ever keep you down...It's good to hear your voice."

"It's too bad we didn't stay in contact, Jack. You left for med school and I for seminary. Then I was gone those ten years. But I appreciate your call. How are things?"

"I've had a couple of setbacks. I'm recently divorced. And I just lost a malpractice case. That was worse. I didn't commit malpractice, but I lost anyway. I know it's nothing compared to what you've been through, so I won't whine. But I do need a change."

"Life has triumphs and defeats. We were supposed to learn that on the football field, but none of us did. Nothing prepares a person for real life. Now, how can I help you?"

"I need to find out if I'm still a real doctor, whether I can still care for people. I'm through with medicine as a business. Can you help me find a place in the missionary field?"

"Jack, we can always find a place for a committed physician. I've got to warn you that our medical expert will evaluate your entire resume, including the malpractice action. I believe you when you say you didn't commit malpractice. It's just we have to credential physicians, just like everyone else."

"I'll be pleased to provide full documentation of everything I've ever done, including the malpractice case. I really want to do this."

"We'll need a sincere commitment. If you just want to run away from home, please don't involve us."

"Please, give me a shot."

"OK, Jack. I'm willing to start the process, but you should take time to consider a step of this magnitude. Send us your résumé only after you really think this through. Of course, you'll have to come to New York for a personal interview. It'll be necessary to convince the missionary society, and me, that you really are ready to give up the career you've pursued all your life, leave your family and friends, take an oath of poverty, and trust God to guide your life. It's not a decision you should make without sober reflection. We can't commit to you unless we know you're committed to our ideals. Committed heart and soul."

"Anything you ask will happen."

"Did I happen to mention your salary will be the princely sum of thirty thousand dollars a year?"

"You mean I get the opportunity to travel and you'll pay me too?"

"When was the last time you lived on thirty thousand dollars?"

"The last time I was happy."

"Where do you want to serve?"

"How about Africa? Preferably somewhere with a few wild animals around."

"There are several possibilities in Africa. It can be a dangerous place, what with the political unrest, AIDS, and other, even scarier, viruses."

"I'd rather live in a place with epidemic AIDS than a place infested with ravenous lawyers."

"If you're sincere God will bless your journey. But I recall you were always somewhat cynical about religion."

"I just want to be a doctor. I won't have to preach, will I?"

"No. We don't have time to give you theological training. If you're a good physician people will come to our clinic. Perhaps, after you've cured their bodies, your clerical brothers will have an opportunity to minister to their souls."

"I'll do a good job for you."

"For God, Jack. Send your résumé, but not too soon. I have a feeling this could be a whim, a reaction to personal life pressures. I know you're sincere at this moment, but are you truly a changed man? A man who lives for others? Pray for guidance. Know this decision will change your life forever. And, Jack, God bless."

"Thanks, Fred. You won't regret this."

Jack hung up. He hoped the Old Testament God of judgment and war would stay with him for the next ten months. Then he'd embrace the New Testament God of peace and brotherhood. Everything in its season.

If there were a God, he must want justice.

CHAPTER THIRTY-SIX

The following Monday Jack returned to work at the hospital. It wasn't a return to a calling, or even a profession. It was a holding action he'd endure for eight or ten months.

He arrived early so he'd have time to check his personal anesthesia cart for emergency drugs and favored equipment. Standing in front of his locker, he realized he didn't remember the combination. Funny how something like that could slip a person's mind. He walked out of the locker room to the charge nurse's desk. She had a master record of all combinations.

The charge nurse, Terri Greene, was sitting at her desk, glaring at the day's operating schedule. The idiot weekend crew, always anxious to avoid quarreling with surgeons who demanded operating room time early in the morning, had added several cases to the list. They hadn't notified her. These add-on cases could never be completed in the optimistic time frame the surgeons predicted. Every surgeon and every patient scheduled thereafter would be inconvenienced by a delayed start time. Terri Greene would spend the rest of her day calming impatient surgeons, distressed patients, and uptight administrators. She knew only one way to handle this situation. Terri determined to establish early Monday morning she was the meanest bitch in the hospital. No one valuing his or her private parts dared challenge her. This always worked.

Jack stood quietly in front of her desk. He waited, but she didn't look up. Finally he said, "Terri, sorry to disturb you. I've forgotten my locker combination. Could you look it up for me?"

Terri approved this humble approach to her throne. She recognized the voice but was unready for the haggard face. "Sure, Doc. I have the list right here. It's usually surgeons who can't remember their combinations, those dumb SOBs. You anesthesiologists are usually just smart enough to remember personal stuff. Ah, here it is. Forty-two, twenty-four, eighteen." She paused. "Jack, I saw what happened in the newspaper. You must know everyone who works with you thinks you got a raw deal."

Jack forced a smile. "We play for high stakes. A person is bound to lose once in a while."

"Doc, you'll get through this," Terri said with genuine sympathy. "We all have confidence in you."

"I appreciate your saying that. I really do."

CHAPTER THIRTY-SEVEN

Jack's operating room behavior changed as he withdrew more and more into his new persona. He gradually became the quietest and least opinionated anesthesiologist on the hospital staff. The quality of his work remained excellent. He spoke to his fellow physicians with constant, almost exaggerated, politeness. His coworkers found him distant, perhaps distracted.

He was distracted. Planning for justice was a challenging mental discipline, something requiring professionalism. He admired professionalism. It was more important to him than money or ego or popularity. A professional used attention to detail, knowledge, and preparation to ensure a predictable result. A professional took no chances.

He began each day with a vigorous one-hour aerobic workout. The physical conditioning forced him to focus on his goal from the moment he woke up. He organized each day to maximize productivity. Time was limited.

All winter Jack devoted his after-work hours to thought, planning, and hardening his will. He waited impatiently for March, when springtime's good weather would allow him to begin intensive physical-skills training.

He began study of a potentially useful tool: the motorcycle. He studied this tool with an intensity he formerly reserved for medical literature. This tool possessed advantages and drawbacks. It was fast and fuel efficient. Its rider could obscure his face with a helmet and his clothing with a protective leather shell. On the other hand, a motorcycle could be treacherous when ridden over wet, rough, or gravel surfaces. To use this tool effectively, Jack would have to acquire new skills and make those skills instinctive. In the final extremity, a hunter acts instinctively, and Jack now thought himself the pure hunter.

Jack knew coordination of his hands and feet on the throttle, clutch, and brakes must be ingrained, requiring no conscious effort. He had to become comfortable in heavy traffic. He must learn to turn at high speed, and, equally important, to balance on the bike at low speed. Heavy rain and irregular surfaces couldn't be limiting factors. For instance, should he be in a pursuit situation, he'd possibly have to cross suddenly appearing railroad tracks at high speed. He considered and vowed to master these and other scenarios.

He decided one of the sleek BMW motorcycles was what he required. They were preferable to something like a Harley-Davidson because they ran quietly, almost silently. He didn't wish to leave a noise signature when exiting an area. Also, the BMW didn't possess any eye-catching chrome or other vanity excesses—paraphernalia a witness might remember. The machine had to be black and his personal riding attire must be dark in color. Whenever possible he'd move at night and use darkness as camouflage. He'd decrease as much as possible the chance anyone could identify him.

He decided a BMW RT 1200 best suited his mission profile. This machine generated one hundred twenty-five horsepower in its six-hundred-pound frame. Its acceleration and top end speed were extreme. It started quietly. It could be accessorized with lockable, aerodynamic trunks of nearly indestructible plastic that attached behind the rider and on each side of the rear wheel. These were nothing like the individualized saddlebags preferred by Harley riders, who tended to be people intent on making a lasting impression.

Jack knew exactly what he required when he entered a BMW dealership the first week of March. A saleswoman approached him. Like many people connected with motorcycle sales, and to her own everlasting joy, her personal passion had dovetailed with her profession. "May I help you, sir? My name is Sophia."

Sophia radiated competence and knowledge. Jack, only too aware of the gaps in his education regarding motorcycles, spoke quietly. "I've wanted a BMW since I was a kid. I've been reading up on things, and I'd like to look at the twelve hundred RT."

"Sir, have you ever owned a motorcycle before?"

"Well, no. But I've always admired them."

Politely pointing out the obvious, Sophia said, "I suggest you start out with a less powerful bike. The twelve hundred is a lot to handle. Could get away from a new rider."

Jack had to progress on a fast curve. "I know I have a lot to learn, but I'd like to begin with the motorcycle I want to ride. If I practice and get good instruction, couldn't I master the skills I need riding the twelve hundred?"

Sophia, serious about her reputation, observed, "It's possible to learn on a twelve hundred. It's a fine motorcycle. But in good conscience, I've got to suggest you start with a less challenging bike."

Jack faced an unalterable time frame. "I'd like to try to learn on the twelve hundred. I promise to attend classes and to follow instructions faithfully. If I can't learn on the twelve hundred, I'll bring it back and trade it for a smaller model. It'll be entirely my responsibility."

She looked at Jack carefully. "I don't need a sale bad enough to set you up with a twelve hundred and have you go out and kill yourself. Bad for my business reputation. How about this? You give me the information I need to order the bike of your dreams. Then you go out and pass a motorcycle safety course. Come back and I'll sell you the bike. But the last part of the program will specify you demonstrate a little competence. My husband will take you to the parking lot and make you ride slowly, turning between cones. Then he'll put you through whatever other exercises he deems appropriate, with no complaints from you. You won't drive off my lot until he's satisfied you won't go out and get yourself whacked. This is the deal-breaking part of our contract. Got it?"

Jack laughed. "Sophia, you silver-tongued devil. Just steer me to your favorite safety course. I'm confident I'll pass. And I'll give you cash for the down payment right now."

Sophia encouraged Jack to order a light-colored bike so he'd be more visible to oncoming traffic. Jack insisted on black, the color he'd always dreamed of. He purchased black leather boots, chaps, and a jacket. He added a dark-gray rain jacket. All the garments were unadorned by slogans, trim, or anything else memorable. He picked out a black helmet, despite her recommendation for the more visible white one, and added a dark visor that was interchangeable with a clear one. Assuring Sophia he'd be back within two weeks for his check ride, he left her shop, pleased with the day's progress.

CHAPTER THIRTY-EIGHT

The following Friday, Saturday, and Sunday, Jack attended a motor-cycle safety course. The motorcycles used in class were Hondas, half as heavy and half as powerful as a BMW 1200 RT.

Jack's advanced age guaranteed his adoption as class mascot by the five instructors and twenty fellow students. He received intense personal instruction because he needed it. His forty-year-old reflexes required extra repetitions for habits to become ingrained. By the end of the class he was considered to be a stiffly mechanical, but probably competent, motorcycle rider. The instructors granted him a diploma along with a warning concerning old dogs and new tricks.

He took his certificate to the DMV on Monday afternoon and obtained a motorcycle operator's permit. That evening he returned to Sophia's motorcycle shop. Sophia and her husband Tim watched as he slid his shiny new license across the counter.

Sophia smiled at him and then looked at her husband. "Tim, this is the older guy I was telling you about. He has that black 1200 RT on order. He probably thinks we'll let him drive it off the lot. Could be he's just a wannabe."

Tim looked Jack up and down. "Maybe. We'll see. Your bike's sup-posed to be here next week. Will that be enough time for you to learn how to handle a big motorcycle?"

Jack said, "I'm in your hands. But I intend to succeed. I've already bought all the cool clothes that go with the bike."

"We'll see if clothes make the man." He gestured for Jack to follow him. In the parking lot gleamed a red BMW. Tim carefully enunciated his words. "This is my personal bike. It's just like the one you ordered, except I have better taste in color. You are going to satisfy me you're not a menace to yourself or anyone else before you drive one of these machines out of here. And, by the way, if you scratch my bike, I will injure you." He gave a sinister laugh.

Tim worked Jack for an hour each evening in the parking lot. He forced Jack to drive over and over on serpentine paths between orange cones, the difficulty magnified by the slow speed. Jack learned to coordinate foot and hand brakes and practiced gearing up and down. Tim discussed the drills Jack had to practice on his own to master higher-speed maneuvers. Jack was an apt student. He didn't scratch Tim's bike.

After Saturday evening's drill Tim said, "Let's go talk to Sophia. Now and then she's been watching you. She's heavily opinionated, and she definitely thinks she's the boss. We'll see if she feels you've made any progress." Tim turned and walked into the shop. Jack, the dutiful student, followed.

Sophia looked amused. "A whole week and Tim's bike is still intact. I made you a deal and you kept your end, so I'll keep mine. Your bike will be here Monday. Give us until Wednesday to get it ready. And after you ride off my lot take some time for general improvement of your limited skills on quiet residential streets before you head off on your first cross-country trip. I really hate it when one of those beautiful machines gets all scratched up."

Jack shook hands with Sophia and Tim. "I'll see you Wednesday. And don't worry, I won't mistreat my bike."

CHAPTER THIRTY-NINE

The following Monday Jack took the Land Rover to the dealer and sold it for considerably less than he thought it was worth. But the money did cover the cost of the BMW. The transaction was more important than the funds received. It symbolized his commitment. Now he possessed an instrument critical for his plans. He'd gain the skills necessary to make that instrument useful by applying the same diligence, determination, and intelligence that had gained him his medical skills.

Jack took a taxi to work on Tuesday and Wednesday. On Wednesday night he took a taxi to Sophia's shop. He carried his helmet and leather jacket in a gym bag. The black BMW was ready. He paid the balance of the purchase price and received last-minute instructions. As he walked out the front door Sophia called to him, "Now don't go out and hurt anyone with that gorgeous bike."

Jack replied, "I'm a physician, Sophia. I'm not allowed to hurt anyone...it's a rule." He placed his gym bag in the top case behind his seat and started the engine. It purred, quiet and powerful. He practiced two hours on city streets before returning to his hotel.

From that moment on he trained with unceasing effort. Expansion of his skills became enjoyable, even addictive. He took no time to evaluate the path he'd chosen. His path was unalterable.

Ten days later a surgeon saw Jack walking into the hospital, his helmet under his arm. "Midlife crisis, Jack?"

"I must have misunderstood you," Jack replied. "What I thought you said sounded like psychobabble."

"The new transportation. Please tell me you still own your car. You'll need it when the snow flies. If you're still alive."

"You never know, my friend. It's a long time until snow flies and things are bound to change."

The surgeon thought, *What a stupid prick.* But he didn't dwell on Jack's mental status. There was money to be made in the operating suite, and, really, what else mattered?

CHAPTER FORTY

Two Saturdays later Jack rode his bike two and a half hours to Kansas City. The trip exhausted him physically, and he vowed to make long trips part of his future training regimen.

Jack rode until he found a decent restaurant in the suburbs. He bought a local newspaper, sat at a booth, and ordered a late breakfast of steak and eggs. Opening the newspaper, he turned to the want ads. Under sporting goods he found the section offering guns for sale. He was pleased to find quite a few private individuals anxious to part with firearms. Today he'd advance his plans significantly. It promised to be a productive day indeed.

He finished breakfast and walked outside. Using a throwaway cell phone, he called the three sellers who possessed equipment he desired.

The first seller wished to part with a drilling, a drilling noted to have a detachable claw-mounted telescopic sight. Jack surmised the woman had inherited a family heirloom. A drilling is a specialized European weapon that breaks for loading like a conventional side-by-side double-barreled shotgun. It differs from conventional shotguns in that it has a center-fire rifle barrel mounted underneath the shotgun barrels. The claw mount allows the telescopic sight to be removed when a shooter utilized the shotgun barrels. When the shooter elected to use the rifle barrel, the claw mount ensured the scope could be reattached with no change in zero. The ad noted the scope was a Zeiss, the shotgun barrels 12-gauge, the rifle barrel 30–06 caliber. A drilling like this was a work of art, a very expensive firearm.

The weapon appealed to Jack. It could be taken apart quickly into a short package of stock, barrels, and telescopic sight. Reassembly for a rifle shot took only seconds. He didn't care what this heirloom cost. He cared about possessing a precision weapon he could break down and carry without arousing suspicion. He made an appointment with the seller for 1:30 that afternoon.

The second offering catching his eye was for a Ruger semiautomatic pistol, .22 caliber, with a four-inch barrel. It came with a second magazine. The weapon had a blued finish, something Jack required. He intended to use the instrument at night, and a flashy, silver, stainless steel model is more difficult to conceal. The seller sounded like a young man. He agreed to meet Jack at 4:00 p.m.

The third weapon on his list was a .45-caliber semiautomatic pistol, a Colt Commander. Its color was the standard dark blue and it came with an extra magazine. Jack had always been impressed with how large and intimidating the muzzle of a .45 appeared when he looked down the barrel. This seller was also a man, but sounded older. He was pleased to meet Jack at 2:45 p.m.

Jack rode the BMW downtown and parked in a city parking lot. He opened the right side touring case and pulled out a large athletic bag containing a carefully folded pair of khaki cargo pants, a three-button pullover sport shirt, and a pair of loafers. He locked his motorcycle helmet in the top case. His leather jacket and chaps went into the left touring case.

He sauntered to a Marriott hotel two blocks away, walked into the coffee shop, and ordered a cup of coffee and a piece of pie. After finishing his dessert, he strolled to the hotel lobby and found the restroom. He entered the last stall and traded his jeans, T-shirt, and boots for the yuppie clothes.

Jack was aware he'd be recognized if the sellers were ever given an opportunity to view a photograph of him. He knew any attempt at disguise would make him appear suspicious. The solution was that the authorities must never find any weapon he used. The identifying serial number would inevitably be traced to the original owner and then to him.

He walked to the front entrance of the hotel and hailed a cab. He tossed his athletic bag into the backseat and climbed in.

The cabby, a thirtyish man exuding disinterest, said, "Where to?"

Jack leaned slightly forward. "The address is 3-0-2-2 Oak Street. It's in a residential district named Buena Vista, about half a mile off I-29. I'm an antique collector, and this is one of three stops I intend to make today. What would it cost to hire this cab and have you stay with me until I get my errands done? It'll probably take until five o'clock."

The cabby asked, "Where are the other two addresses?" Jack read them to him. "The addresses aren't close to each other. You'd have to pay the usual mileage fare and then give me a generous tip. Like two hundred bucks."

Jack smiled into the rearview mirror. "That's steep, but I need to get this done today. The antique shop doesn't run itself and I need to be at work early Monday morning. So I'll give you a hundred bucks now and a hundred bucks more plus the usual fare when we finish and you drop me off here. Deal?"

It was an unusual request, but the yuppie in the backseat looked harmless enough and had money to blow. "Deal." The cabbie reached back to collect the first hundred dollars.

The cabby tried light conversation as he drove to the first destination, but it became apparent his fare wasn't interested in small talk. He decided to just drive. Let the guy in the backseat think about money for a while. That's all guys like him worried about anyway.

The cab reached the first address at 1:20 p.m. and pulled into the driveway to wait. Jack walked to the doorway and rang the doorbell. A small woman in her fifties opened the door. Jack smiled pleasantly and said, "My name is Barry Mathews. I called you earlier today regarding a firearm you advertised in the newspaper."

The woman seemed uncomfortable. She looked Jack over carefully. "Is your cab going to wait for you?"

Jack continued to smile. "Well, yes it is, ma'am. I buy and sell antiques as well as classic firearms. I have several errands to run, so I've hired the cab for the afternoon. I hope you don't mind his waiting in your driveway, but I do have to be efficient today."

The woman, relieved, said, "No, I don't mind a bit. Come in. I'm not that comfortable with guns. My father recently passed on. He left several guns. Most we sold at a sporting goods shop, but the owner of the shop said this remaining gun was rare and only someone knowledgeable would recognize its value. He believed he'd have trouble selling such an expensive gun and suggested I run an ad in the newspaper." She paused. "He said the gun is worth forty-five hundred dollars."

"Ma'am, I have to look at the gun before I can determine what it's worth to me," Jack replied laconically. "Remember, in my business a firearm is only worthwhile if I can sell it for a profit."

"Please wait right here." She left Jack in the entryway and walked to an adjacent room. She returned with a hard leather case approximately three feet long, two feet wide, and a foot thick. She indicated Jack could follow her to the living room. She placed the case on a low table.

Jack looked at the woman. "May I?" She nodded and he opened the case. Inside was a drilling with an exquisite walnut stock. He took the barrels in his left hand and grasped the stock with his right, then snapped the barrels into place. The action closed with a solid sound like the closure of a bank vault. He picked up the telescopic sight, a Zeiss variable power instrument with magnification of 4X to 12X. He checked the claw mount, and then seated the scope on the barrels. Everything had the feel of precision equipment.

The woman looked at Jack. "It's worth forty-five hundred dollars."

Jack needed this weapon. It could be carried broken down, transported, reassembled, then deliver a precision shot. He kept a straight face. "That may be true, ma'am. But I do have to make a profit. For me, it's a business. I'll give you thirty-five hundred dollars. Right now. Cash."

The woman said, "The other guy told me it's worth forty-five hundred."

Jack sighed. "I have to point out it's not worth anything to you hidden in a back room of your house. This is a specialty item. Very few people appreciate it and fewer still can afford it. I'm offering you cash right now. I'd be willing to bet this item has been on the market awhile, but most potential buyers back off when they hear the price."

133

Her eyes told him his last statement was true. She looked away. Finally she said, "I'll sell it to you for forty-two hundred dollars. I'll include a box of rifle bullets and a few shotgun shells my father left behind."

Jack handed her the drilling. He smiled and told her he had to be on his way. She stopped him.

A few minutes later he walked out of the house, the leather case in his left hand, a paper sack of ammunition in his right. He was thirty-eight hundred dollars lighter.

Jack walked to the cab, opened the right rear door, and slid the case to the left. He got in and shoved the paper sack into the athletic bag. The cabby watched him in the rearview mirror. "Whatcha got there?"

Jack looked out his window, plainly bored. "A set of antique silverware. At least she packed it in that old leather case. I'm sure I'll find some sucker who'll take it off my hands and make me a few bucks. Make sure you don't go around any corners too fast. Don't want this stuff rattling around."

The cabby was pretty sure a leather case was an unusual container for silverware, but he looked at Jack's face and decided it would be unwise to investigate further. He drove for half an hour to the second address and arrived at 2:35 p.m. He parallel parked on the street. Jack looked at the house and said, "I'll just run up to the door and see if the guy will see me early. Keep an eye on my purchase, will you?" He got out, slung his athletic bag over his shoulder, and walked to the house. He felt confident the cabby wouldn't get too curious.

He rang the doorbell. A potbellied man in his sixties answered. Jack said, "I'm the guy who called about the .45."

The man, relieved his customer wasn't an obvious desperado, said, "Come in. I've got the gun right here." He handed Jack the original box with a Combat Commander pistol inside. "I have an extra magazine. I haven't shot it much. I bought it for self-defense several years ago, but found I couldn't hit a barn from the inside. Now that we have grandchildren around the wife wants it out of the house."

Jack opened the box. He held the pistol up, worked the action, locked the slide open, and looked down the barrel. He'd bet the pistol hadn't actually fired more than one box of shells and had probably never been cleaned. The action was slick, the sights good. It was serviceable. "How much do you want for it?"

The man said, "I paid seven hundred dollars for it, and I'd like to get my money out."

Jack stared at the pistol in his hand and said, without looking up, "The piece has never been cleaned and it's been sitting dirty in the box for years. The barrel's filthy and may not be accurate. I'll give you three hundred bucks for it."

The seller became self-conscious. His customer had hit the nail on the head. He didn't know how to clean the damn thing, and he didn't want to deal with any more customers. He also didn't want to be nagged by his wife anymore about what a dumb thing it had been to buy a weapon, and how he'd be forever responsible if harm came to a grandchild. "Done."

Jack put the pistol back into the box and shoved it into the athletic bag. He pulled out his wallet and extracted three hundred-dollar bills. He held the money up and the man's stubby fingers closed around them. "Thanks."

Jack voice was flat. "A pleasure." He slung his bag over his shoulder and walked out of the house.

Jack got back into the cab. "Let's see if we can finish early. How much time to the next address?"

"Forty-five minutes."

"Let's go."

They reached the last house at 3:40 p.m. A man in his twenties answered the doorbell. Jack said, "I called you earlier about the Ruger .22. I'm early, but hoped you'd be home, this being the weekend and all."

"Sure thing. Come on in." Jack entered and closed the door. The man indicated Jack could sit on a couch in what appeared to be a family room, the first room left of the entryway. The man ran up a flight of stairs and came back immediately. The .22 was in his right hand, two empty magazines were in his left. The pistol was empty, the slide opened and locked.

Jack accepted the weapon when the youngster offered it to him. The young man said, "I hate to part with it, but I'm a little short right now."

The pistol was clean, well cared for. Jack said, "I believe you said you wanted two hundred fifty dollars for it."

"Yes sir."

"It's worth it." Jack pulled out his wallet and handed the seller five fifty-dollar bills. He pushed the pistol and magazines into his athletic bag.

Jack started to the door. From behind him he heard, "Have a nice day." He raised a hand in a wave without turning around and walked to the cab.

The cabby looked into the rearview mirror as Jack dropped into the backseat. He commented, "You sure must like small antiques. You walk in and walk out with that bag and it doesn't seem to get any bigger."

Jack looked directly into the mirror. "I have a real good idea. Why don't you take me back to the Marriott by the most direct route?"

The cabby looked into Jack's green eyes, which had somehow assumed the coldness of a hunting cat. He decided he wasn't curious about this man.

The taxi pulled up to the Marriott entrance. Jack held up four hundred-dollar bills. The cabby wanted to speak to fill the silence, which suddenly seemed profound. "That'll do it," he said.

Jack stepped out of the cab, slung his bag over his right shoulder, picked up the leather case with his left hand, and walked away without turning around. As Jack walked through the hotel entrance, the cabby felt relieved. He pushed the money into his pocket and drove away. He'd had enough for one day. He'd go to his favorite bar, have a drink or two, and go home.

Jack walked through the lobby and straight into the rest room. He changed clothes and shoved his yuppie uniform into the bag. He slung the bag over his shoulder, picked up the gun case, and walked to his BMW in the parking garage. He took the helmet out of the top carrier, set it down next to the bike, then put the athletic bag into the left touring case. With four bungee cords, he secured the drilling behind his seat.

He dressed in his leathers, pulled his black helmet on, saddled up, and started the BMW. He looked forward to the night trip back to Omaha. No one intruded in the darkness.

Jack drove the two and a half hours back to his hotel and parked in his assigned space. The athletic bag remained in the touring case. He went to his room, hid the drilling in his large clothes hamper, and hoped any potential thief wouldn't have time to thoroughly search the room.

He fell asleep as soon as his head hit the pillow—the sleep of the just.

CHAPTER FORTY-ONE

Ammunition for the drilling came with the weapon, but Jack lacked bullets for his newly acquired pistols. After securing ammunition, he'd familiarize himself with his tools. The most private place he knew to evaluate weapon function and dependability was the farm where he'd deer hunted the past few years. He must make sure each weapon's sights were properly aligned—in the language of shooters, zeroed. Then he planned to oil each weapon and place it, with its ammunition, in a separate heavy plastic bag. The land had innumerable hollow logs and brush piles, ideal places for hiding his weapons. No one was likely to visit the forest until hunting season rolled around in the fall. He'd fulfill his destiny before then.

Jack had to destroy his weapons when their usefulness ended. Ridding himself of the two run-of-the-mill pistols was no problem. But the drilling—a product of the best old-world craftsmanship—was another matter. He'd regret it. Jack smiled when he thought of how his psychiatrist friends would react to this. He was planning murder and his major regret was the destruction of a weapon.

Jack considered his target list. Each person on the list was guilty of the same crime. They were willing to destroy him for money. In some cases, not even a lot of money. Each had acted out of personal greed. None of them sought justice. They believed Jack was weak, incapable of seeking retribution. Every person involved in Jack's destruction was sure they'd get away with it. For them it was a game, and Jack happened to be the loser.

Well, maybe it was just a game. The problem for these people was they hadn't anticipated how rough the game could get. They prided themselves on being ruthless and tough. They deserved to be intro-duced to the next level in the game of life.

Jack thought about his ex-wife. Kate had used him skillfully and become personally wealthy. She planned to collect more winnings until both their daughters passed eighteen years of age. She'd gained much with a cynical seduction. Kate hadn't deserved what she'd taken from Jack, and she didn't deserve to collect more of his money over the next ten years.

Finally, Jack excluded Kate from the list. The girls needed their mother because soon their father planned to depart on an extended trip. Kate would likely never figure out she was still alive because of the girls. Even if she gained that knowledge he doubted she'd become a better mother.

The following morning, Sunday, Jack slept until ten o'clock. He caf-feine loaded himself with a can of Diet Coke, grabbed his workout bag, and headed for the gym. He couldn't miss his physical conditioning two days in a row. Being in shape made him confident. It gave him an edge.

After a vigorous aerobic workout and a luxuriant shower, he went to his favorite restaurant to enjoy a meal of steak, eggs, and hash browns. Not a meal designed for someone interested in longevity.

He rode the BMW to a local indoor shooting range, an establish-ment catering to yuppie shooters. The range rented handguns to shooters in the hope a well-heeled customer might discover a hand-gun he couldn't live without.

Jack had frequently shot at this range. As always, he carried a small bag containing his hearing protection and shooting glasses. The pro-prietor and Jack were on a first-name basis. "Jack, coming in to while away a Sunday afternoon punching holes in targets? You're lucky. We aren't too busy today. There's several lanes open."

Jack smiled and shrugged. "That's great. Thought I'd shoot a little with one of your .45s. Then maybe I'll finish up with some work with a .22."

The proprietor was solicitous. "You'll have a good time. Who knows? Maybe you'll have such a good time you'll actually buy one of my guns instead of just renting them."

"I still can't make up my mind about handguns," Jack replied. "Growing up on a farm we shot a lot of rifles and shotguns, but no one could afford to buy a handgun. Guess I'm experimenting with pistols now just to broaden my horizons."

"So what'll you want today, Jack?"

Jack studied the pistols displayed on shelves behind plate glass. "Let's see. How about one of your 1911 Colts? I've always liked the feel of that model in my hand. Then maybe I'll try one of the Ruger .22s. Want to make sure I'm not flinching when I get done shooting the .45."

The owner removed two pistols from the case and made a show of checking that each was empty. He locked each slide in the open position and placed the weapons on top of the counter on a black mat. "How much ammunition do you want today?"

Jack looked thoughtful. "I've got plenty of time. Give me three boxes for the .45 and two boxes for the .22."

The owner took the bullets from a shelf behind him. A good share of his profits came from selling ammunition, and it was good stuff. He permitted no one to bring his or her own bullets to his shop. This ostensibly ensured a shooter never fired a round that might penetrate the bullet stop at the back of the range. It was just good business.

The owner laid the boxes of ammunition in an open-topped shallow plastic container, maybe twice as large as a shoebox. It wasn't an unusual quantity of ammo. A serious shooter could easily expend that many bullets in a single target session. And the doctor seemed to be an interested, and probably above-average, shooter. The owner then placed the two pistols in the container next to the boxes of shells. "Anything else, Jack?"

"No, that'll do. Be out in an hour or so." He pulled on his protective glasses and earmuffs and picked up his equipment. He walked to the door of the range and entered.

Jack strolled behind the other shooters on the range, nodding as he passed by. He entered the last firing lane. A wall was on his left. He put the box containing his equipment on a counter. Each lane was designed so a shooter stood between wooden partitions reaching from floor to ceiling. This prevented a shooter from being struck by the hot brass ejected from a semiautomatic handgun fired in the adjacent lane. The partitions also hid anything the shooter did on his counter from his neighbor's vision. No one could watch Jack unless he stood directly behind him.

Jack hit a button and the target holder automatically came forward from the far end of the range, twenty-five yards away. It stopped directly in front of him. He attached a paper target with a single bull's-eye six inches in diameter. He never shot at a target representing a human torso. Jack wanted to give any observer the impression he was interested only in competitive target shooting.

He pushed the reverse button and the target moved back down the lane. After it traveled ten yards Jack pushed the stop button. The target swayed softly back and forth, eventually coming to a stop.

Jack picked up the .45, ejected the magazine and, in no great haste, pushed seven short, thick bullets into it. He liked .45 caliber ammunition. The bullets were large and ugly and looked like handgun bullets should look.

He pushed the magazine into place. The visual picture he wanted came immediately into focus as he assumed the handgun Weaver stance—pistol held in the right hand with the right arm nearly straight, pushing the barrel right at the target. His left hand gripped his right hand with the left arm bent to ninety degrees. The left hand and arm pulled the right hand-the gun hand-down so the recoil of the shot wouldn't lift the muzzle of the pistol. The muzzle had to be kept down so the shooter could reacquire the visual picture necessary for a quick, accurate second shot.

Jack felt solid. The front sight was in sharp focus, centered between the blades of the rear sight. He focused intently on the front sight. The rear sight and the target were slightly out of focus. He slowly squeezed the trigger and the gun discharged its slug downrange. His left hand pulled downward on recoil and the front sight raised only a little. It remained on the bull's-eye. He squeezed the trigger two more times and then let the muzzle drop to a forty-five-degree angle to the floor—the ready position. For the first time since the firing sequence began

Jack shifted his visual focus from the front sight to the target. There were three holes in the black.

Jack slowly fired the remaining four rounds into the bull's-eye. He started moving the target back two yards at a time. He expended two boxes, one hundred rounds, of ammunition. Accuracy began to degrade at sixteen yards. At twenty-four yards he struck the bull's-eye six times out of ten shots. He wasn't an expert pistol shot, nor had he time to become one. But he was adequate at close, very personal, range.

No one was behind Jack. He dropped one box each of the .45 and .22 bullets into his shooting bag.

He loaded ten rounds into the magazine of the 22, placed a new target on the frame, and ran the target just five yards downrange. Assuming the Weaver stance, he fired three evenly spaced shots in three seconds, and then lowered the pistol to the ready position. The .22 caliber holes in the target were tiny, and all were in the black. Jack continued shooting three-shot groups as he slowly backed the target out two yards at a time. At thirteen yards, the group of tiny holes remained in the black, although the group was growing progressively larger. At fifteen yards, fliers began missing the black bull's-eye completely. By the time the target reached twenty-five yards, half the rounds were in the black and half were in the surrounding white paper. For a few fleeting moments Jack entertained the thought of practicing several times weekly so he could achieve genuine handgun accuracy. He rejected that thought. It wouldn't do to gain a reputation as someone who practiced with a handgun frequently.

The inevitable conclusion was he'd have to get close to his targets. Real close. But that was OK. He wanted to be close. He wanted these people to understand how personal this was. His opponents thought themselves invincible. He wanted to look into their eyes and see how they reacted to the game when it advanced to the next level.

He finished the box of .22s. Just inside the entrance to the range the owner had stationed a broom and dustpan. Jack used them to clean up all his spent cartridges, which he dropped into the plastic garbage can used as a receptacle for brass. It was impolite to make anyone pick up for him. More importantly, he didn't think anyone needed to know how many bullets he'd actually fired.

He walked off the firing line and returned to the front counter. He laid his shooting bag on the glass case and pushed his shooting glasses and ear protectors inside. The proprietor looked up at him. "How'd it go?"

"Well, you know," Jack said in the self-deprecating voice farm boys used to deflect criticism, "I'm really not that good. Every time I try this, I realize how difficult it is to shoot a handgun."

"Oh, come on, Jack. If you showed up here once a week you'd probably shoot like Dirty Harry."

Jack laughed. "I'll have to think about it. I've just about reached my frustration limit. I'll come back when my self-esteem returns."

The proprietor smiled a little too easily. He presented Jack with the bill for the range time, ammunition, and gun rental. Jack paid in cash. He waved to the proprietor as he left the establishment.

He never saw the proprietor or the gun range again.

CHAPTER FORTY-TWO

Jack returned to work Monday, performed a week of competent work, didn't hurt any patients, and waited for the weekend.

Early Saturday morning he packed the BMW. First he opened the left touring case, took out the athletic bag, removed his yuppie clothes, and took them to his room. The athletic bag, with its contents of recently acquired handguns, the box of 30-06 bullets, and the half box of 12-gauge shells, went back into the case. He returned from his room with his shooting bag containing his recently purchased handgun ammunition. This went into the right case along with a gun-cleaning kit, three spray cans of gun oil, a sack of linen patches designed for cleaning gun barrels, and a small tool kit. He filled the top case with a box of heavy-duty garbage bags and a tarp, military green in color. Finally, he strapped the drilling's leather case behind his seat and covered it with a gray rain slicker, then secured that bundle with clothesline.

He began his ride to a farm forty miles south of Omaha. The farmer had undergone successful coronary artery bypass surgery six years previously. Jack had performed his anesthesia. During Jack's postoperative visit the farmer learned his anesthesiologist was an avid hunter. With genuine appreciation for the care he'd received, the farmer invited Jack to take a deer or two, and maybe a wild turkey, from the three hundred acres of hardwood forest he owned along the Missouri River. The two became friends, and Jack was a regular visitor in subsequent years.

Jack pulled into the farmyard at 8:15 a.m. A German shepherd, whose existence centered on protecting the farmstead, interposed himself between the farmhouse and the strange helmeted man riding the motorcycle. Jack, moving deliberately, removed his helmet and leather jacket. He knelt on one knee and opened his arms as if greeting his best friend in the world. "Lobo, don't you recognize me?"

The dog responded to the familiar voice. He bounded to Jack, tail wagging, and laid his head against Jack's chest. Jack fussed over him, making Lobo feel like the most loved dog in the world.

"That dog sure does like you." Jack looked up to a woman in her sixties, a woman who combined an air of toughness with unmistakable feminine charm. Martha, the farmer's wife, was rumored to be the real boss of this piece of real estate. She smiled. "Looks like you have a new vehicle. Glad old Lobo decided to allow you to identify yourself before he took vigilante action. He's kind of aggressive when Jacob's gone."

Jack stood up. "Beautiful day, isn't it? How've you been?"

"It's been a good spring. Corn and beans are already up. Fact is, Jacob's out cultivating corn right now. I've just made some cinnamon rolls and fresh coffee. Why don't you step in?"

Jack thanked Martha and they went into the house to her kitchen. They made small talk, and each ate two cinnamon buns, still warm from the oven. Nothing ever tasted as good as warm rolls in a well-lit farm kitchen.

Martha started to clean the table. She waved Jack off when he offered to help. "Well, what brings you out here today? It's a little late for spring turkey hunting, isn't it?"

"Unfortunately it is. I got so busy I missed the whole turkey season. Hope to do better next year. Anyway, I've got a couple of guns packed in that motorcycle and wondered if I could go back to the timber and sight them in."

"Go right ahead. Jacob is in a field two miles north of here. He's nowhere near the timber, so you can fire away." She laughed. She treated men and their guns the same way she treated children with new Christmas toys.

"Thanks, Martha. I'd better get going because I have to get home before dark. I don't want to surprise a deer on the road at night and ruin a perfectly good motorcycle."

Jack thanked Martha again at the door. He walked to the BMW, stopping on his way to pet Lobo. He pulled on his jacket and helmet and drove away from the farmstead. Half a mile away he turned left on a dirt lane that led to the Missouri River.

Jack followed the dirt lane, driving slowly. It hadn't rained for a week, which was fortunate because the BMW, for all its virtues, wasn't a dirt bike. He stopped where the lane wound between two hills. The hill to his left rose sharply and was covered with short brush and a few small, insecure trees. The hill to his right rose in a more gradual manner and was populated by a grove of mature oak trees. The large trees had shaded out the smaller vegetation, making it possible for Jack to set up targets up to three hundred yards away with good visibility. The hill was steep enough to ensure an effective backstop for the bullets. Jack hoped that shooting in a hollow between two hills would trap, or at least muffle, the sounds of his weapons. He didn't want any curious onlookers to wander onto his range. They might ask questions.

Jack took a paper target and some fine wire from his shooting bag. He stretched the wire between two trees, and then attached a target to the wire with binder clips. The bullets would impact on the ground between the trees. It was unconscionable to fire bullets into oak trees aged a hundred, or maybe two hundred, years old. Ancient trees like these would stand long after people's fleeting lives had ended.

Jack took out the .22 Ruger and loaded both magazines. Five yards from the target, he fired three shots in a slowly measured cadence. The weapon cycled well. He stepped back to ten yards and fired all the bullets contained in both magazines. There were no feeding problems. Accuracy was adequate. He was satisfied with the pistol.

Next he picked up the .45. He filled both magazines with seven rounds. He emptied each magazine into the target, the first magazine at five yards, the second at ten. The weapon fit Jack's hand well and was a pleasure to shoot. He placed all the bullets into an area the size of a pie plate at five yards. At ten yards, he placed five of seven rounds into the same area. Therefore, in Jack's hands, this pistol was serviceable to ten yards. It would do.

Jack placed the handguns back into the luggage carrier. He walked a hundred paces from the dirt lane and set up another target. Returning to the BMW, he unstrapped the leather case and assembled the drilling. He rolled up his raincoat to make a pad to rest the forestock of the weapon, then lay down into the prone position, carefully placing the drilling on its improvised rest, making sure there was no pressure on the barrels.

He set the telescopic sight up to maximum magnification, 12X, and looked at the target through the scope. The sight picture was clear and bright. He rolled onto his left side, opened the weapon, and inserted a 180-grain soft point 30–06 cartridge. He turned again into the prone position and sighted carefully at the one-inch diameter circle in the middle of the target. Through the powerful scope Jack could observe his heartbeat throwing the crosshairs off the tiny target. Heartbeat—crosshairs above the target—relax—crosshairs settle back on target—heartbeat—crosshairs off target again. He'd shoot when he knew he should—between heartbeats.

He settled on the target. Nothing mattered except the target and the crosshairs bisecting it. He squeezed the trigger between heartbeats. Recoil, which forced his shoulder backward, took his vision off the target for a split second. Because he'd taken the recoil straight backward and had not allowed the muzzle of the rifle to rise, he was back on target immediately. He could see the one-inch black target circle and the place where the bullet struck.

The bullet hole was four inches high and three inches to the left of the bull's-eye. The previous owner had fired the weapon enough to get the telescopic sight close. Jack adjusted the scope after each subsequent shot. Three shots later he observed a neat .30 caliber hole two inches above the black circle. According to ballistic tables this rifle should therefore hit dead-on at two hundred yards and about a foot low at three hundred. Of course, he'd have to proceed scientifically to ensure calibration of the rifle. Calibration was necessary for any precision instrument.

Further testing demonstrated the rifle was dead-on at two hundred yards and fourteen inches low at three hundred. Jack knew he could hit a pie plate, or a human torso, out to three hundred yards. Every time.

Jack took the scope off the drilling and dropped a twelve-gauge shotgun shell in each of the two shotgun barrels. He picked out two rocks, one fifteen yards away, the other thirty. He fired the left shotgun barrel at the first rock, the right at the second. The hail of shotgun pellets discharged from each barrel pushed the rocks into the soft dirt. The old-world craftsman who had created the drilling had produced a masterpiece of versatility and effectiveness.

Jack disassembled and cleaned each of his weapons. He wiped away the residue resulting from the discharge of the cartridges and applied oil to all metal surfaces. He pushed oil-laden patches through each barrel. Obsessive attention to detail prevented rust—the enemy of accuracy—from forming.

Jack placed the drilling back into its leather case, reassembled the .22, and then pushed each weapon into a separate garbage bag. He emptied his remaining .22 shells into a ziplock bag and did the same with the twelve-gauge shotgun ammunition and the 30–06 cartridges. He put each ziplock bag in the garbage bag holding the appropriate weapon. Finally, he tied the garbage bags shut and rolled them into the green tarp.

The still-disassembled .45 and its cartridges remained on an open garbage bag ten feet from the BMW. He decided he'd keep the .45 with him. He divided the component parts of the pistol into three separate ziplock bags. These went into his motorcycle tool kit with the belief that no one would examine his tools closely. He zipped his remaining .45 bullets into his motorcycle jacket and vowed not to get himself picked up for some stupid traffic violation.

Jack picked up the ungainly tarp-covered load with both hands and headed for his destination in the woods.

Five hundred yards away lay the hollow trunk of a huge, long-dead maple tree. Jack had eaten many midday lunches sitting on top of the old giant. He found the tree as easily as an urban shopper walked to her car in a mall parking lot and was gratified to see it hadn't disintegrated. He crawled into the hollow trunk, pushing the tarp and its contents ahead of him until they rested six feet from the entrance. He spent the next few minutes arranging fallen limbs over the trunk's opening, and finally, stood back to satisfy himself that he'd left no sign of his activity. Then he slowly moved away, making sure he left no trail.

He returned to the BMW by an indirect route, picked up the paper targets, crumpled them into a pile twenty yards from the motorcycle, lit them with a match, and watched them burn. When every scrap of paper had been consumed, he stomped the smoking ash and kicked it about, leaving no sign of a fire. He recovered the wire for disposal in a garbage can at some gas station on the way home.

He walked the hills for a couple of hours, his exercise discipline for the day. He marveled that birds sang, squirrels ate acorns, and deer lay alert and still despite the recent gunfire.

It pleased him that no one had wandered down the lane to investigate his shooting.

He slowly rode his motorcycle up the lane and out of the woods. His maturing riding skills allowed him to control the heavy bike on the slow uphill climb.

He stopped at the farmhouse and was immediately greeted by Lobo. Martha stood on her front porch, smiled, and nodded toward the barn. Jacob, a big man whose huge forearms belied his sixty-two years, walked to Jack. Jacob tilted his green John Deere cap slightly back on his forehead with his left hand and reached out to shake hands with his right. "We've missed you, Jack. Those turkeys are getting overconfident because no one chased them this spring. Probably eat us out of house and home. You'd better get after them next spring or there'll be nothing left on this farm."

Jack smiled. "I'm not entirely dependable. One of these days you'll have to shoot one or two of those birds yourself."

Jacob laughed. "Then I'd have to go out and buy shotgun shells and one of those camouflage outfits, and I'd probably have to sit under some tree during a spring rainstorm. I think I'll just leave all that hard work to city folk who don't know better. I'd rather continue growing my food in a civilized manner. Why don't you come in and drink some lemonade and visit a few minutes before you head out...Say, don't you know most folks grow out of the motorcycle stage after they leave high school?"

The three of them spent half an hour drinking lemonade and talking about everything and nothing. The farm couple, in the best rural tradition, didn't pry into Jack's unusual behavior. But a motorcycle? For a doctor? The conversation remained lighthearted and happy.

Jack stood up. "I've got to get going. I have a Technicolor picture of some deer stepping out of a ditch at night and hesitating in front of the motorcycle. Would make quite a bump."

The couple stood up. Jacob said, "You be careful, hear? Stop in and see us soon."

"You know me. I'm like a bad penny. Just keep showing up."

Jack walked to the BMW, put on his jacket and helmet, and waved as he drove away.

Jacob and Martha looked solemn as they waved back.

CHAPTER FORTY-THREE

Jack began frequenting Omaha's downtown area. He visited it on his days off and in the evenings after work. He became familiar with the shopping areas, the business district, the coffee shops, and the cafés near Ben Harris's law office. Once Jack spotted Harris entering a bar at eleven in the morning. A grim thought crossed his mind. *Probably that's where he was when he should have been preparing me for my deposition.* Several times Jack observed Harris's office lights on until after eight o'clock, long after his secretary had left for the day. The good counselor Harris seemed to enjoy working at night alone. This indicated the lawyer preferred reviewing legal precedents with a bottle in hand, something impermissible if his secretary or clients were present. It also explained the attorney's inability to function before noon.

Two weeks into his surveillance, Jack followed Harris home. For the occasion he rented a beige Ford Taurus. It would be too obvious to follow anyone, even a drunk, at night with a single motorcycle headlight. The target left his office at 7:30 p.m. and drove home with meticulous, almost comical, observance of traffic laws. He obviously didn't think it wise to speak with a police officer in his current condition. Harris led Jack into a section of town with tree-lined streets and older middle-class homes. Jack drove by as the garage door opened. He meandered around the neighborhood to identify parking spaces and escape routes. He intended to return to this area only one more time.

The next day after work, Jack returned the rental car. He paid the bill in cash.

Two days later Jack left work at four in the afternoon. He worked out for an hour, as was his routine, then stopped at a nearby café. He ate the steak dinner special in a booth close to the cash register and read the newspaper as he dined alone, just as he had on numerous occasions in the past. The waitress received thirty dollars for the twenty-two-dollar meal and was pleased with the tip. Jack waved at the café owner as he exited through the front door.

Jack walked to his hotel room and changed into a denim shirt, jeans, and his black leather coat. He buckled on the final part of his attire, a black leather fanny pack. Inside were the Colt .45, cocked and locked, two pairs of latex gloves, and a 10 cc syringe capped with a one-and-a-half-inch twenty-two-gauge needle. The syringe contained forty milliequivalents of potassium chloride.

The front desk clerk, Mrs. Hanna, supplemented her social security check by working at the hotel from two until ten o'clock, four days a week. She gave Jack a grandmotherly smile as he entered the small lobby. "Dr. Andrews, out again for one of your evening joyrides. Really, a doctor should be wise enough to avoid riding one of those infernal machines, particularly at night."

Jack liked Mrs. Hanna and didn't have to fake his smile. "You know, after a tough day in the operating room, nothing settles my nerves like some time on the bike. I just love cutting through the darkness on such a fine machine."

"You be careful, Doctor. Don't want to be reading about you in the newspaper tomorrow."

"Mrs. Hanna, no one wants to avoid being in the newspaper more than I do."

Jack walked to the garage and donned his black helmet. The unconventional doctor with the eccentric habits was at it again.

As the early summer's twilight faded, Jack parked the bike on a street outside a heavily wooded park at 8:45 p.m. The sign said the park was closed from 11:00 p.m. until 6:00 a.m. Plenty of time. He locked his jacket and helmet in the motorcycle's top case.

He took a black baseball cap from inside his shirt and pulled it low over his eyes. It was maybe half a mile to the lawyer's house, a leisurely fifteen-minute walk. He hoped Ben was home.

He walked down tree-lined streets at a moderate pace and nodded pleasantly to two dog owners walking their pets. People were out enjoying a beautiful spring evening.

Jack turned up Harris's driveway and walked to the front door with the confident manner of a long-lost friend. He rang the doorbell and turned the fanny pack to the front, unzipping its top compartment.

Ben Harris, irritated and bleary-eyed, opened the door. He had a glass in his hand. Recognizing Jack, his irritation turned to indignation. "What are you doing here?"

Jack spoke very quietly. "I just wanted to speak with my former lawyer. You know, professional to professional."

Harris's alcohol-soaked brain registered alarm. He reacted with lawyerly aggressiveness. "If you have something to say to me, make an appointment at my office. Now, get out of here. You have no right to come to my home."

Jack spoke even more quietly. "Look here." Harris followed Jack's eyes and he found himself staring at the butt of the .45 that Jack's right hand had eased out of the fanny pack just enough to be visible. "Ben, old boy, if you make any noise, I'm going to put two slugs in your chest. If you want to live, open the door and let me in."

The glass fell from Ben Harris's hand. He took two steps back. Jack took two steps in and pushed the door shut with his foot.

Jack pulled the handgun all the way out and pointed the muzzle at the lawyer's eyes. He wanted Ben to appreciate how large the pistol was. "If you lie to me, things won't go well. Is there anyone else here?"

Ben looked at the muzzle. "No one's here. I live alone."

"Just you and your bottle, right? Lie down on the floor facedown. You and I have to talk." Harris complied awkwardly. He was grotesquely out of shape. Jack stood perfectly still and listened. If anything moved in the house, he wanted to know. He waited a full minute. Harris started to mumble something. Jack said, "Shut up." Harris shut up.

After what seemed an eternity to the man facedown on the floor, Jack stated, "I have come to believe no one could be as incompetent as you were when you handled my deposition. I think you must have set me up for Carl Hafen. You made sure I looked guilty and did nothing to help me. Did you and Carl split fees? Were you working together?"

Harris started to talk in an emphatic voice. He denied the charge. Jack rumbled, "The next time you talk loudly, I'll kill you. I want a quiet professional discussion. None of that noisy lawyer bullshit."

Harris next spoke in a low ingratiating voice. He was determined to talk his way out of this. Then he'd get the cops on this son of a bitch, this arrogant doctor. Did a physician think he could assault an officer of the court? "Look, Doctor, you may not feel the advice I gave you was good enough, but I had to work with the facts as I knew them. I had no deal with Carl Hafen. Do you think I'd jeopardize my license? Think of that, Doctor."

Jack sighed. "Well, I don't know if you're telling the truth. I don't trust you. So I brought along a little Pentothal. You know, truth serum. I'm going to find the truth. Everyone knows people don't lie after they've been injected with Pentothal."

Harris had heard of Pentothal and he grasped hope. He'd let this stupid fool give him the drug. Of course he hadn't had a deal with Hafen. Carl would never trust an alcoholic, damn him.

Harris suddenly had a terrible thought. What if he said something about calling the cops as soon as the SOB left? He'd concentrate on not telling the cops. That's what he'd do. Then he wouldn't blurt out anything about turning this idiot in. This doctor, this fool, could run his little lie detector test. He'd even the score soon. Certainly he'd make a lot of money in the civil trial that would follow the criminal conviction. This doctor must have some money left somewhere, and he'd get it.

Jack said, "Now listen carefully. You're going to turn over. You don't have an intravenous line running, so I'm going to stick a needle into your neck and inject the Pentothal. It works best if it's injected close to the brain." That made sense to Ben Harris. Had to get the drug to the brain. "Now, turn over and take the stick. I promise you it'll be just one stick. If you're telling the truth, I'm out of here. If you move, I'll shoot you."

Harris turned over onto his back. Jack said, "Keep your arms at your sides. Turn your head a little to the left. That's it. Now, don't move."

Jack was kneeling at Harris's head. Harris couldn't see him well. He heard a snapping sound as Jack pulled on latex gloves. "Have to maintain sterility, even for a piece of shit like you."

Jack placed his left hand on the right side of Harris's neck and palpated the landmarks. He reached into the fanny pack with his right hand and took out the syringe. He pulled its cap off with his teeth. "Hold still," he ordered. "I don't want to put this in the wrong place."

Jack placed the tip of the needle into the lawyer's right internal jugular vein. Harris was amazed that the stick was nearly painless. Jack pulled back on the plunger of the syringe and demonstrated free flow of blood. He injected the contents of the syringe, forty mills of potassium chloride. Jack pulled the needle out cleanly and carefully laid it two feet to the side of Harris's head. He pushed on the puncture wound with his gloved hand.

Ben Harris felt his heart begin to pound. This wasn't the feeling he'd expected from Pentothal. He thought he'd feel relaxed, sleepy. But he had very little time to evaluate the strange feeling. Ten seconds after Jack injected the potassium chloride Harris's heart simply stopped. He was in cardiac arrest. All circulation of blood ceased. No oxygenated blood reached his brain, which died in just a few minutes.

Jack kept pressure on the needle stick site. He didn't want any blood leaking into the tissue to alert the medical examiner. Since there now was no blood circulating, he decided five minutes were enough. He lifted his hand away. There was no swelling. Good. Jack wasn't worried about a postmortem test discovering the potassium. After death, all cells secreted potassium as they broke down. Toxicology tests would show nothing. A meticulous dissection of the right internal jugular vein might find the needle stick, but Jack counted on the likelihood that the overworked and unsuspicious medical examiner wouldn't be interested in undertaking such time-consuming effort.

Jack picked up the syringe, recapped the needle, and put it back into the fanny pack. He saw a drop of blood had fallen from the end of the needle onto the floor. He wiped this up with the latex gloves, then took the gloves off and pushed them into the fanny pack. The .45 followed. He pulled on the second pair of latex gloves and examined the body. There was no hematoma or black-and-blue discoloration. The small needle hole was not directly over the external jugular vein, which would have been the obvious target of a less experienced doctor. In fact, the small nick looked as if it had been caused by a shaving mishap.

Jack examined the scene intensely. Had he forgotten anything, left any clues to his presence? He hadn't. Ben Harris was a morbidly obese man in his forties, and a drunk. He'd had a heart attack in his entryway as he'd passed by with a glass of booze. Jack doubted anyone would be sufficiently interested in Ben Harris to investigate his death thoroughly.

Jack looked out the window. No one was on the street. He walked out the front door and shut it with his gloves on. With his back to the street he pulled off his gloves and stuck them in his front pocket. He walked leisurely, but not directly, to the park and was standing beside his bike at 9:55 p.m. He put on his helmet and jacket. The BMW, its engine quiet, eased slowly onto the road. He rode on a series of streets to a county highway he'd frequented during his motorcycle training sessions. Ten miles out of town he turned onto a gravel road and traveled two miles. He stopped and ensured he was alone, then took a copy of the day's newspaper from the left touring case, crumpled it on the road and lit it on fire. He dropped the gloves and syringe on the small blaze and they immediately melted. He threw the needle into the ditch.

He took the pistol from the fanny pack and put it in the touring case. He filled the pack with large stones. It was always possible some blood had leaked out of the syringe needle into the pack, just as it had on Harris's floor. DNA testing is conclusive in court so the pack had to go. Between Jack's current location and Omaha, the county road crossed the Fox River, a tributary of the Missouri. Jack stopped on the bridge and threw the fanny pack into the water. There was a satisfying splash.

Half an hour later, and still on a gravel road, Jack disassembled his handgun while holding a flashlight in his teeth. He distributed the parts as he had before in his toolbox. The bullets went into his jacket pocket. He'd hide them in his hotel room.

One down, he thought.

CHAPTER FORTY-FOUR

The next morning, Saturday, a sleepy Dr. Jack Andrews reported to the hospital at seven o'clock to begin his twenty-four-hour in-house call responsibility. He read the Saturday newspaper between cases and listened avidly to the news reports broadcasted hourly over a golden-oldies radio station piped into the operating room. No one mentioned any diminution in the local population of attorneys. He managed to sleep the last four hours of his shift, from three to seven, then rode back to his hotel and read the Sunday paper. Still no mention of any prominent deaths in town. Jack slept a few hours, worked out, and spent the rest of the day in his regular routine. He was gratified no one seemed interested in his whereabouts.

On Monday Ben Harris failed to appear at his office. His long-suffering secretary, used to his absences, rescheduled his few appointments. She didn't call him. It had become tiresome listening to excuses for his hung-over days off. She closed the office at five o'clock, hoping the drunk would show up on Tuesday.

Tuesday morning at ten o'clock the secretary called her boss at his home. He had two appointments in the afternoon and probably needed a couple hours to clean up. She spoke loudly to the answering machine, demanding Harris pick up. He didn't.

The secretary became worried for the first time. What if something were actually wrong? What if her boss had fallen down the stairs while drunk? He had no friends who would check on him. She called 911.

Two uniformed police officers knocked on the door. They noted a distinctly foul odor and looked at each other. One of them found the doorknob unlocked and pushed the door open.

There, lying on the floor, was Ben Harris, esquire. A broken drinking glass was next to his body. He was on his back, his facial color ranging from dark blue-gray closest to the floor to a uniform gray around his eyes and forehead. He'd been dead a long time. The younger officer, a rookie, leaned in and got a full whiff of the premises. He ran to the middle of the yard, fell to his knees, and vomited.

The older officer, more experienced and possessing a stronger stomach, called headquarters and requested an investigation team. He told the sergeant there was no hurry.

Michael Weber, one of the more experienced detectives on the force, arrived forty-five minutes later. The medical examiner had already initiated his investigation. So far the doc knew for sure that Mr. Harris was very dead and had been in that state for several days. The body was bloating, sagging, and demonstrating signs of extreme deterioration. The medical examiner expressed happiness he'd missed breakfast because, "It wouldn't have tasted good a second time." Of course he'd do an autopsy. Just as soon as his stomach calmed down. He didn't see any evidence of foul play, but he'd call Sergeant Weber in a day or two.

The investigation team found no evidence of forced entry. They began a search for evidence of burglary, but didn't expect to find anything.

Mike Weber asked a team member if Ben Harris had any known enemies. The team member had no idea, but reminded Weber that the decedent was, after all, a lawyer. Weber commented, "He was a lawyer, huh? That narrows the suspect list to about half the people in town." Both men laughed.

Weber reviewed all information concerning Harris's death as it came in over the next week. No neighbors had heard or seen anything. It was obvious no one thought anything was amiss because the body had lain unattended for three days. That length of time also indicated no one would miss the deceased.

The autopsy was performed hurriedly by an overworked medical examiner who found nothing to indicate foul play. The coronary arteries demonstrated mild hardening, but not to the degree usually associated with a heart attack. The ME concluded Ben Harris, who had been drunk, had experienced an irregular heartbeat which had progressed to a cardiac arrest. Unusual but not unheard of.

Weber conducted a background check into the deceased's life. He found no one who expressed anger, surprise, or even curiosity about this citizen's death. Ben Harris was put in the ground and forgotten. His faithful secretary found another job within three weeks.

Jack read an obituary in Wednesday's newspaper. It described the death of a local attorney, Ben Harris, attributable to natural causes. At first Jack was elated. He'd done it and gotten away clean.

Then he came back to reality and settled down. He must remain the consummate professional, never be betrayed by emotion, never make a mistake, never get caught. His society had denied him justice, but he would have it. He would win.

CHAPTER FORTY-FIVE

Jack began his surveillance of Carl Hafen. Hafen was Harris's polar opposite. He worked hard, always arriving at his office early and leaving late. He dressed well but not flamboyantly. He drove a spotless older-model Mercedes. He exuded competence, control, and ruthlessness. Hafen enjoyed the good life and was willing to destroy anyone to keep his lifestyle humming. Jack was familiar with this personality type.

Ten days after Ben Harris's death, Jack had lunch in a diner across the street from Hafen's office. He sat in a booth, baseball cap pulled down over his forehead. Busy people hurried in and out of the diner, all of them too self-absorbed to notice or remember him.

Jack had finished eating and was ready to signal the waitress for his bill when his target walked in. Walking behind Hafen was a woman in her twenties, his secretary. Jack recognized her from his time in court. Holding her hand was a man of approximately her age. The man looked familiar. Who was he? Another patron came through the door. The hand holder turned to look behind him. As he turned his face Jack recognized him. He was a hospital janitor, a man Jack had often seen in the OR. Jack hadn't recognized him because he was attired in casual clothes, not the scrub suit he wore in the OR. *Expensive clothes for a janitor*, Jack thought.

Jack waited until the party of three strolled to a booth in the back of the diner. Their path didn't pass Jack's booth. He left money for the meal, including a decent, but not remarkable tip, and walked out with his head down and his hands in his pockets.

He walked four blocks to the BMW in deep thought. He remembered a surgeon who only infrequently operated at Jack's hospital. Jack had remarked in casual conversation that he hoped to work with the surgeon more often. The surgeon had replied, "I only work at your hospital when the patient specifically requests it. It makes me nervous to work in a place where the biggest plaintiff's lawyer in town has an informant."

"What are you saying?" Jack was surprised. "Who around here would do anything like that?"

"One of the janitors in your operating room is married to the secretary of a plaintiff's attorney," the surgeon responded. "The wife attended one of those hospital family picnics with her hubby. The dumb bitch was shooting the shit with a group of nurses and told them where she works. The law office of Carl Hafen. That prick. Of course, no one can go after hubby and move him out of the OR. Civil rights and all that. But I don't believe in coincidences. Guys like him work in the background and don't say much, but they hear a lot of things. I don't know anything for sure about the guy, but I operate elsewhere whenever possible."

At the time, Jack had dismissed the allegations as the usual surgeon bombast. Now he began to rethink the issue. How had Carl Hafen selected him as his target? Did he have some insight into Jack's psychological state? How did the patient's family settle on Hafen as their attorney? How could Hafen, who never did anything that didn't benefit him financially, have time to take his secretary and her janitor-husband to lunch? How could the janitor dress so expensively? Would Hafen, who was seriously into personal wealth, pay his secretary enough to afford such things just because he was a nice guy? As the surgeon said, there were no coincidences.

Late the next night Jack drove south of Omaha to retrieve the .22. He didn't stop to see Jacob and Martha. He parked his bike in a driveway that led off a gravel road to a cornfield. This time of year there was no fieldwork that required a farmer to be out at night. Jack cut through the cornfield to the familiar forest and walked directly to his downed maple. He used a small Maglite as he crawled into the hollow trunk to recover the .22 and its ammunition. He rewrapped the drilling, crawled out, turned off his flashlight, and returned to the BMW.

Back in his hotel room, Jack was gratified to find the .22 not rusted and in perfect working condition. He wiped excess oil from the outer surfaces of the pistol and passed several dry patches through the barrel to remove every trace of oil within. A barrel can produce accuracy only if it's clean and dry. He hid the pistol in the pocket of a heavy overcoat in his closet, ready when opportunity appeared.

Jack had learned one important characteristic of the .22 caliber cartridge during his boyhood on the farm. When it had been necessary to put down an injured pig or steer in the feedlot, his father had always pushed the muzzle of the rifle right against the condemned animal's head. This muffled the sound of the shot so other animals weren't frightened by a sudden noise. Jack didn't have a suppressor on this pistol, but, if possible, he'd use the same trick to silence his shot.

Five nights later Jack left work a little after eight o'clock. He decided to unwind by going downtown and cruising on the BMW. He rode by Hafen's office at 8:35 p.m. and noted the lights were still on. Carl had new reputations to ruin. Jack parked a block away and slipped into an alley where he could watch the entrance to Hafen's business. It was dark and probably dangerous in this downtown alley so late in the evening. This was excellent insurance no one would interfere with him.

Half an hour later, Hafen appeared on the sidewalk speaking into a cell phone. In another five minutes a Mercedes pulled curbside. Hafen opened the passenger door and slid in. The Mercedes pulled away slowly and drove away on an almost-empty street. Jack hurried to the BMW and followed at a considerable distance.

The Mercedes traveled less than a mile before entering the parking lot of the Lark, a high-end steakhouse. Jack rode by.

He went back to his hotel room and changed into black jeans and a black T-shirt. He took the .22 and the ziplock bag of cartridges from their hiding places. After donning latex gloves, he wiped each cartridge clean with a rag. With the gloves still on, he loaded the two magazines. One magazine he pushed into the pistol, then jacked a round into the chamber. He put the weapon into a black fanny pack. The second magazine and another pair of latex gloves went into the right cargo pocket of his jeans. A black ski mask went into the opposite cargo pocket. He put on his leather coat and dropped the ziplock bag of remaining bullets into a side pocket and closed the zipper. Lastly he crammed a black baseball cap into the opposite side pocket. It was time for his appointment at the Lark.

He rode the bike to a poorly illuminated parking space four blocks from the restaurant and secured his helmet in the top case. Jack walked to the Lark, baseball cap pulled low. He moved through the night and became part of the darkness.

The Mercedes was still there. One other car was in the parking lot. No one was on the street. He dropped down and sat with his back to a delivery van a hundred feet from Hafen's car. At 10:55 p.m., a man and woman Jack didn't recognize left the restaurant. They walked to a Lexus, the woman looking anxiously into the darkened lot. The car started and sped away. Jack stayed completely still...

After the second shot, Jack stayed low, squatting. Nothing moved and nothing made a sound. He replaced the .22 in the fanny pack and took the latex gloves from his pocket. He pulled the gloves on and took a Rolex watch from the dead man's wrist. From the woman he took a bracelet, a necklace, and a very nice watch. The jewelry went into Jack's left front pocket. He retrieved Hafen's wallet, emptied it of perhaps two hundred dollars, and dropped it on the ground. The woman's purse contained only a few dollars stuffed in a side pocket. She obviously didn't make it a practice to pay for things herself. Jack dumped the purse's contents on the pavement between the two bodies. The money went to the same pocket as the jewelry.

Jack looked around, alert. Nothing happened. The entire exercise had required less than three minutes. He stood up and walked into the shadows. In darkness he took off the latex gloves and ski mask, pushing them into the cargo pocket of his jeans. He took the baseball cap from the jacket pocket, pulled it low over his face and walked slowly away.

Just as he reached the bike he heard the first sirens in the distance. He unlocked his helmet, put it on, started the BMW and cruised away. He took a direct route out of town and violated no traffic laws.

He'd been happy to educate Carl Hafen. At long last Carl had learned to take something personally.

CHAPTER FORTY-SIX

The young blond woman, whose name was Tiffany, awoke fifteen minutes after receiving the head blow. She groggily got to her hands and knees and crawled a few feet. Her vision began to clear. Something nearby caught her attention. Carl was sitting there, staring straight ahead. Tiffany began to scream. She screamed louder and louder. Lights came on inside the Lark. The owner, truly frightened, called 911 immediately. Only then did he look out his front window.

Jack rode the BMW south out of the downtown area to the Thirteenth Street ramp and then onto I-80. Heading east, he crossed the Missouri River into Iowa in less than ten minutes. On the north side of Council Bluffs he took the exit to Highway 6 and continued east. Seventeen miles later he crossed a bridge over the West Nishnabotna River. Neither farmhouse nor traffic lights were visible. He rode slowly over the bridge, stopped momentarily at its midpoint, and threw the .22, the extra magazine, and the jewelry into the water.

He turned right at the next gravel road and rode several miles until he found a place where the road went down a steep hill and immediately began a steep incline. No lights were visible—it was after midnight in rural Iowa. He put the BMW on its kickstand, took the remaining .22 bullets from the ziplock bag, and scattered them in the high grass growing in the ditch. Inside his right touring case were two pages of newspaper and a lighter. He crumpled the newspaper, lit it on fire, and added the money from his front pocket, the latex gloves, and the ziplock bag. Everything was transformed into light ash, which he scattered with his feet.

Jack started back to his hotel room, enjoying the solitude of a quiet ride home.

CHAPTER FORTY-SEVEN

At 2:05 a.m. Sgt. Michael Weber slowly opened his eyes and glared at the ringing phone. He picked up the receiver and immediately recognized the voice of the chief of police. "Mike, I need you right now. One of our more prominent citizens just got whacked. He got it in the parking lot of the Lark, of all places. He's a lawyer, Carl Hafen. Do you know who he is—ah—was?"

Weber, instantly awake, responded, "I've heard of Carl Hafen. A big-time plaintiff's attorney. What happened?"

"Some guy just walked up and popped him. Shot him point-blank with a .22. Most likely the first shot was in the spine, dropping him. Then he took another round right through the heart. Patrol found brass from both rounds."

"How do you know it was a man? Did someone see him?"

"Yeah, Mike, we have a witness. Hafen was with his girlfriend. She saw the guy do it. At least she saw the first shot. Then the guy hit her with something and knocked her out. Broke her face all up, the bones around her right eye. When she wakes up, she sees Hafen. He's sitting up against the car. Dead as shit."

"Chief, does this Hafen have any connections or enemies who'd want him killed?"

"Mike, he was a lawyer. A plaintiff's lawyer. He made his living attacking people with money and prying it away from them. So you can bet there are at least several people out there angry with him. On the surface this looks like a professional hit. You know, a .22, close range, well-placed shots. What's puzzling is everyone who knows Hafen says he didn't deal with drug dealers or anything like that. He didn't need to. He took his money from respectable members of our community."

Mike Weber paused, considering. "If this guy got hit by a pro, why did the girlfriend survive? It's hard to believe a pro would leave a witness, someone who'd seen him shoot this guy. And why didn't he finish Hafen with a head shot?"

"I don't have the answer to that, Mike. Maybe we have a hitter with a conscience."

"Maybe we have someone with a personal grudge. And why was the body sitting up? Is it possible there was conversation before the second shot? If the victim was just shot—bang, bang—he should be flat on the ground." Weber paused. "What'd the shooter look like?"

"We could interview the witness for only a few minutes before the ambulance took her away. All she could remember seeing was this man appearing out of nowhere. She said he didn't make a sound, he was like a ghost. And there he was, right next to them. She couldn't see his face. Probably had a ski mask on. Dressed all in black. He just materializes out of the dark. Doesn't say a word, just shoots Hafen. At least she thinks he shot Hafen. Apparently the noise wasn't as loud as a gunshot in the movies. So, she thinks there was a shot. Hafen starts to fall, but she doesn't remember seeing him hit the ground. She does remember the ghost start to turn toward her. She wanted to scream. And that's all she remembers until she wakes up next to the corpse."

Weber became philosophical. "I'll bet some guy who emerges out of darkness seemed supernatural. She says he didn't say anything? Didn't try to rob them?"

"No, Mike, not a word. Just bang, you're dead. He did take Hafen's watch and the lady's jewelry and the cash from their wallets. But he didn't threaten them first."

"Did anyone else see anything?"

"We're doing interviews. The restaurant owner called 911. Hafen and his lady were the last customers of the night. The owner waved good-bye to them and then went about shutting the place down. Next thing he knows, maybe twenty minutes later, he hears screaming outside. Calls 911. He grabs the guy doing books in the back room. They go out, real cautious, and walk to the screaming. They find the lady and the corpse. Then there are a lot of red lights, and the first patrol car pulls up. The two restaurant guys were only too glad to see the cops. But they didn't hear or see anything until the screaming started."

"Chief, the guy was waiting for Hafen. Hunting him. He gets an opportunity, he takes him. I don't understand why he didn't make everything clean by killing the witness. Doesn't make sense. No one believes this was a robbery, right?"

"Not a robbery. Too well done."

"Chief, I'm on the way. We better get a team together first thing tomorrow. We've got to find out who Hafen's been fooling with. Need to check all his lawsuits for the past four or five years. We'll have to know if good old Carl was secretly messing with drug dealers or other assorted bad guys. And we better find out if he slept with the wrong woman."

Mike Weber started dressing. He lived for this stuff.

CHAPTER FORTY-EIGHT

Jack reached his hotel at 2:45 a.m. The clerk nodded to him as he crossed the lobby. He was a strange one, this doctor, always riding his motorcycle in the middle of the night. Oh well. Everyone knew you had to be a little strange to spend your life in an operating room where they cut people open.

Jack sat down in his room and stared out the window. The cops were going to review all of Hafen's records, and they'd come to his name. They'd discover Jack had a connection with both Carl Hafen and Ben Harris, two recently dead attorneys. The connection would excite them. They'd take a very hard look at Dr. Jack Andrews.

He laughed at the irony. This was the game he wanted to play. The cops would conclude he was a murderer, but they had to prove it. The same legal system Carl Hafen and his stable of so-called experts had used to enrich themselves now worked to Jack's advantage.

He had to be careful, had to make sure the cops never found hard evidence implicating him. He'd play the game more effectively than the people who'd attempted to destroy him. His enemies had mistakenly believed the game was limited to destroying professional reputations and making piles of money. They'd been arrogant and foolish. Jack Andrews was neither of those things. He never took anything for granted.

The cops would start watching him soon. Unlike many of his so-called intellectual friends, Jack believed the cops were smart. And tough. And dedicated. They liked the game. Soon, proving Jack guilty would become someone's favorite new game.

He must finish soon. The next several days were critical. The cops might put things together rapidly. He couldn't allow himself to get caught. It was unthinkable he be displayed as a trophy for some district attorney, a district attorney who had made the world safe for legal extortion. Jack considered death preferable to such a fate.

CHAPTER FORTY-NINE

T he next morning's newspaper contained the obituary of Carl
Hafen. Whoever wrote it had described the deceased in more virtu-
ous terms than Jack thought appropriate. The funeral service two days
hence, Saturday morning at 11:00 o'clock, was to be held at a local
funeral home. The mourners would follow the casket to Woodhaven
Cemetery for burial. Participation in mourning was by invitation only.

Woodhaven Cemetery lay in a beautiful valley on the eastern edge
of Omaha. The cemetery itself was situated on the north side of the
Flint River, a tributary of the Missouri. A high bluff on the opposite
side of the river was covered by a state forest more than six hundred
acres in size. It was a stunning setting for a cemetery. A mourner could
look up from a loved one's grave and contemplate the dense hardwood
forest ascending from the south side of the riverbank. To a thoughtful
person this small treasure of nature might represent the unending
cycle of life.

It was, in fact, a largely undisturbed area with only one long loop-
ing trail. Many people remarked at its beauty, though few walked
through it. Almost no one remembered there was a forest here only
because the land on the south side of the river was simply too steep for
development to be economically feasible.

Friday night Jack left his hotel room at eight o'clock, late enough
to ensure it would be dark when he reached Jacob and Martha's farm.
He reached the dirt lane leading to his hunting area and rode to a
point out of direct sight from the road. After shrugging on a small
black backpack, he began the hike to his maple.

Movement was slow in the dark, and it took half an hour to reach the downed tree. He packed the drilling into his backpack in three pieces—the barrels, the stock, the scope—each wrapped in a towel. He placed four 30–06 cartridges and four 12-gauge shotgun shells in the outside pocket of the pack and zipped the pocket shut. All other ammunition went into the backpack's main compartment with the weapon. He shoved the tarp as far into the stump as he could, then pushed the drilling's fine leather case in against it. Weather and rodents would destroy the hand-tooled case in short order.

His route back to the BMW led by the bank of the Missouri River. He threw all the ammunition in the pack's main compartment far out into the current and listened as each shell made a splash.

He reached his bike half an hour later and put the backpack into the top case. There was enough moonlight for him to ride on the dirt path and then the gravel road without light. A quarter mile after reaching the hard-surfaced road, he flipped his headlight on and traveled directly to Omaha.

CHAPTER FIFTY

J ack parked the BMW in the hotel garage at 2:30 a.m. Saturday. He ensured no one was in the vicinity before he began execution of the plan. He couldn't waste time. The state forest was four miles away, and he had to reach it before the sun came up. He put his leather jacket into a touring case and his helmet into the top case. Jack's attire consisted of a dark green long-sleeved cotton shirt pulled over a gray Chicago Cubs T-shirt, olive-green cargo jeans, and brown hiking boots. In one pocket of his cargo jeans was his black ski mask, and in the opposite pocket was a pair of latex gloves and a washcloth. He shouldered the compact backpack and walked out of the garage and down the street toward the Flint River. This hike would be less challenging than his usual exercise routine.

Just before sunrise, Jack entered the trees. Moving quietly, he left the main trail and hiked downward to approach the river, avoiding any damp or muddy areas where he could be easily tracked. He walked on rocks whenever they were available and slipped through the thickest vegetation. Jack blended with his environment. He spent more time observing his surroundings than he did moving. He was a predator.

He worked in a downstream direction until he saw a tent in the cemetery. It marked the burial spot.

Jack worked around a limestone cliff. He located a niche where vegetation shielded him from direct view, but allowed a clear field of fire to the tent. The range looked to be three hundred yards, but the straight line to the target was steeply downhill. Bullets fired downhill always struck higher than predicted due to the vagaries of ballistics. The telescopic sight was dead-on at two hundred yards. He therefore decided to place the crosshairs just above where he intended the bullet to strike.

He assembled the drilling, and, from the zipper pocket of the backpack, withdrew two 30–06 bullets and two 12-gauge shotgun shells. After donning the latex gloves, he wiped each round clean with the washcloth. He inserted the shotgun shells, intended only for an emergency should he be surprised, and one 30–06 bullet into the drilling. The second rifle bullet was laid on a prominent rock to his right. He created a rifle rest from rocks and his backpack and set the telescopic sight on maximum magnification.

He looked at the tent through the scope. The sight picture was bright, clear, and steady. Now he would wait.

At 12:45 p.m. a hearse appeared on the winding road to the tent. Following was a procession of luxury automobiles. A man with somber clothes and the serious demeanor of a funeral director exited the hearse. Two assistants followed him. With understated gestures they directed the invited guest mourners to their appointed stations near the grave. Six men walked alongside the casket as it was transported on a wheeled cart to the grave site.

A minister in clerical collar and black robe stood in front of the crowd. He looked absolutely sincere.

Jack, moving his head slowly, looked all around his position, ensuring he was alone. Then he scanned the crowd. There was much more involved than simply locating his target. No one must be standing directly behind him. It would be inexcusable to shoot through his man and kill an innocent bystander. Jack hated sloppiness.

At long last the well-dressed target moved to the right side of the crowd. Next to him stood his equally well-dressed wife, the secretary. No one stood behind them. They were keeping a respectable distance from the VIPs.

He put the crosshairs on the man's face and studied it. The crosshairs dropped to a point even with the target's collarbones. Jack felt calm, still. It was as if he were directing himself, not a bullet, to the target.

The explosion of the cartridge came as a surprise to Jack. The target went straight down into a sitting position, his back to a gravestone.

Jack could see blood spreading from an entry hole in the upper abdomen, dead center but perhaps six inches lower than he'd expected. It didn't matter. The expanding bullet had gone through the aorta or vena cava. Blood cascaded out. The target stared straight ahead, gasping. His wife leaned down, mouth open, staring into her husband's eyes.

Jack broke the weapon open, extracted the spent cartridge, placed it automatically into his right front pocket, pushed the second bullet into the chamber, and closed the weapon.

He corrected for the six inches of unexpected drop in trajectory of the first bullet and steadied the crosshairs just at the top of the secretary's head.

The last thing the janitor ever saw was his wife's head exploding in a red spray.

Every individual around the grave site was now lying low. A few curious people were peering around, but most of the witnesses kept their heads low, staring at the ground in front of them. A woman looked up from her prone position and screamed. A man grabbed her shoulder and forced her head down. He put his hand over her mouth to quiet her, stared into her eyes, and shook his head vigorously. She sobbed and reached to touch his shoulder. Another man called out, "Keep quiet. Don't move. Don't attract attention to yourself."

Jack broke the drilling down and pushed it into his backpack. He began to move upstream, always staying away from the established trail, and always remaining in the heaviest undergrowth. A cornfield extended to the fringe of the forest a quarter mile ahead. He knew he'd leave tracks in the field, but the corn plants extended upward higher than his head and no one could observe his movements directly. He had to cross the field quickly, had to vanish before the police picked up his trail.

He walked through the cornfield until he came to the gravel road he knew lay on its opposite side. He leaned out from the last row of corn and made sure no witnesses were nearby, then pulled off his outer long-sleeved green shirt and shoved it into the backpack. The gray Cubs T-shirt, now wet with sweat, was underneath. It would dry quickly on this hot August afternoon. He pulled the baseball cap from his cargo pocket. The cap was red with a large white *N* on the front. Jack was now one of about ten thousand people in Omaha wearing the ubiquitous University of Nebraska tribal clothing.

He crossed the wire fence and walked in the overgrown ditch. In less than fifty yards the mud was scoured from his boots, and he climbed to the gravel road. Two minutes later he turned right on a hard-surfaced road. One hundred yards away was a residential area of established houses and tall trees. The area had been developed long ago because of its proximity to the forest and the view of the river. Its residents were used to students at the nearby high school and community college carrying backpacks as they hurried to class. Jack kept his head down, avoiding eye contact with the few people he met, as he walked at a steady but unhurried pace. As he continued to move away from the cemetery, he heard the distant wail of sirens.

After clearing the residential area he stowed the Nebraska cap in the backpack. Never know, some witness might recall seeing a man with a Nebraska cap walking through the neighborhood adjacent to the forest. He didn't need to have another person remember, "Oh, my gosh," that Jack Andrews was wearing a similar cap when he returned to his place of residence.

Two hours later he reached the parking garage, removed his leather jacket from the left touring case and shoved the backpack in. He zipped up his jacket, pulled on his helmet, and headed straight out of town.

He had to destroy all physical evidence. He'd soon be a suspect. Conviction was certain if anyone discovered proof linking him to the crimes.

His own attorney in his malpractice case had invested a lot of time training Jack to stay calm, to avoid cracking under close interrogation. Soon it would be determined if his attorney had been truly skillful in creating an effective liar.

CHAPTER FIFTY-ONE

Jack rode east on I-80 into Iowa and on to Des Moines and then turned north on I-35. He exited at Story City to buy gas at a Casey's General Store. He walked into the store to pay, and, in what seemed to the attendant to be an afterthought, picked up a bag of Match Light charcoal. He lugged the bag outside, extracted two bungee cords from a pocket of his leather jacket, and secured the bag between his seat and the top case.

Jack crossed the interstate highway on a hard-surfaced county road and rode east and north on a series of such roads. He turned due north on Highway 65, and, just after 8:00 p.m., entered the business district of Iowa Falls. Continuing north, he came to a small motel. It barely survived on a highway twenty miles off the interstate. He parked his BMW out of the direct vision of a gray-haired man who was sitting in the office and watching an old movie on television.

Jack put on his best smile and went inside. "Hi, sir, I hope you've got a room available. It's going to get dark soon, and, with all the deer in these parts, I'm afraid to ride my motorcycle any farther. Those deer make motorcycling kind of dangerous at night."

The old man nodded thoughtfully. "Those darn deer. Didn't have any for years, but now they've just about taken over the country. Wreck more vehicles and eat more corn than all the other varmints combined. Could use something to thin them out. The hunters don't do nearly a good enough job. But you're in luck. We have several rooms open. Be thirty-nine ninety-five a night plus tax."

Jack looked relieved. "That's great. I'll pay in cash, if that's all right."

The old man beamed. "Much prefer cash. Could you fill out this card?"

Jack wrote the name William Sherman—one of his favorite Civil War generals—on the card and made up an address in Lincoln, Nebraska. Then he looked imploringly at the old man. "I always forget my license plate number. Should I go out and check it?"

The old man laughed. "At this time of night? Mister, I couldn't care less. Here's your key. You're in room one thirty-four. I gotta tell you, I'm going to bed at ten. If you need anything better get hold of me before then."

Jack removed the backpack from the left touring case, then a heavy-duty garbage bag containing clothes and a shaving kit from the opposite side. He threw the backpack over his left shoulder, tucked the garbage bag under his right arm. and walked to room 134.

Upon reaching his room, he took off his clothes and stuffed them into the backpack. He tied his boots, with the tread police could identify from the cornfield, onto the outside of the pack. He dressed in blue jeans, a black T-shirt, and black socks. He set his second pair of boots, a different brand with a different tread than his original boots, near the door. The wait began.

The three-hour wait was the most difficult thing he'd done all day. He disciplined himself to remain still, convinced the police had not had time to connect the dots. Premature action on his part could lead to disaster. He had time to do this right. His legal opponents had used a long delay prior to taking him to trial as a tool to increase his fear and make him question himself. He'd lost self-confidence and become vulnerable. Timing of an action is essential for effective strategy. He'd move only when the time was right.

At midnight he moved. The old man's light had been off since 10:30. The light from the glow of a television in a room four doors down, the last light in any of the motel units, had gone off at 11:10. Jack looked out at the parking lot and the road beyond. He watched for ten minutes, and then slipped into the darkness wearing his backpack.

He stopped at the BMW, untied the charcoal, tucked it under his arm, and began walking down the highway. Turning left at the intersection with the first gravel road, he walked another half mile then crossed the ditch, entered a cornfield, and proceeded between rows of tall green corn for several minutes. It was utterly dark in the field, and he'd have been lost but for the knowledge he had only to follow the rows of corn to reach the end of the field.

He knelt on the ground, took the Maglite from the front left pocket of his jeans, opened the bag of charcoal, and lit it with a match. As the fire rapidly spread, he laid all three components of the drilling on the rapidly heating bed of charcoal. The wooden stock slowly began to burn. Jack fed the clothing he'd worn that day, the Nebraska baseball cap, and the backpack into the flames. Finally, he laid the boots on the charcoal bed. From his right front pocket, he recovered the four unused shotgun shells, the two unused 30–06 cartridges, and the brass from the two expended rounds. He threw them as far as he could.

He slipped away from the fire at 3:00 a.m., making no attempt to put it out. He wanted the heat to continue working on the barrels. It would destroy the weapon's bluing so rusting could begin immediately. Rust would destroy the rifling in the barrel, making it impossible to match a recovered bullet with this particular gun. There had been a recent rainstorm and there was no possibility the fire would spread. Already all that remained was a tiny yellow flame almost invisible in the ashes. No one would visit this spot until harvest began a couple months from now. By that time leaves from the dying corn plants would cover the remaining metal, and the combine harvesting the corn would pass over without the operator noticing what lay on the ground. It was possible, but unlikely, that the farmer would find the rusty barrels and scope the next spring when preparing the ground for planting. By then Jack Andrews would be gone.

Jack was back in his room by 4:05 a.m. He'd seen no one. He washed his hands and face, brushed his teeth, and grabbed his shaving kit, jacket, and helmet. Twice, he checked the room to make sure he'd left nothing behind. Leaving the key in the door, he began his trip back to Omaha.

He'd been allotted one more day of life and never so appreciated the beauty of a sunrise.

Jack Andrews had settled comfortably into the new role of consummate predator.

CHAPTER FIFTY-TWO

Michael Weber received a call within an hour of the deaths. A young detective, speaking rapidly, described a spectacular hit. "It was Carl Hafen's burial service at Woodhaven Cemetery. There were two shots and two people are dead, Hafen's secretary and her husband. We believe the shots came from the state forest across the river from the cemetery. Witnesses agree the shots came from that direction. We're organizing a search. We'll be looking for tracks or the weapon or any other evidence."

"Were you been able to cordon off the park?"

"After we sorted things out we attempted to seal off the park, but the hitter had time to exit. The first patrol cars responded within three minutes and went straight to the cemetery. There was so much confusion and panic that it took time to get credible witness accounts. And it took time to check the dead, to make sure there were no more casualties, and to dispatch ambulances. Then patrol units were sent to block the park, but unless the guy was incompetent he had time to get away."

"Does this guy seem incompetent to you?"

"No, sir." Long pause. "But we do have a helicopter on station now."

"Yeah, that'll help a lot. Just have those guys fly around and look for anyone walking around carrying a rifle…Sorry, I shouldn't talk like that. I'll be there ASAP. Have the guys triangulate where they think the shots came from. Tell them to look especially for tracks or pushed down vegetation. Also look for things he might have used, like water bottles or food wrappers. Don't fuck up the crime scene."

Weber arrived forty minutes later and walked to a bench situated near the prospective burial site. He stared at the forest across the river.

It had taken careful planning to pull this off, but the shot wasn't so difficult that it required a trained sniper. It required good, not necessarily great, shooting.

Weber mused about the hitter. Obviously, someone had a grudge against Carl Hafen and his associates. This person required extreme retribution, and he had to deliver it personally. Someone was settling a score.

Hafen had made a fortune assassinating the professional competence and character of highly successful individuals, the kind of people who had risen in life with hard work and sacrifice. One of those people hadn't accepted the old lawyer's dictum that it wasn't personal, it was just business. That someone had taken things very personally indeed.

Weber would review Hafen's legal victims. Someone would stand out, someone who could kill. Not many people fit that mold. Lots of people say they want to kill another person, but very few carry out the act. Murders like this required specific skills and more nerve than the average citizen possessed.

A young patrolman jogged up. "Detective Weber, we found boot prints exiting the park. We followed them through a cornfield to a gravel road. We can follow scuffs on the gravel, but they lead to a hard-surfaced road. We lost him there. But we have casts of the boot, and we're searching the path, looking for a weapon."

"How big are the tracks?"

"They were left by an average sized guy. Maybe size ten or eleven."

Weber said, "Tell everyone to look everywhere in the cornfield, not just along the path. We have to find that rifle." A voice in the back of Weber's mind said, *They aren't going to find the rifle. Or anything else.*

CHAPTER FIFTY-THREE

Jack returned to his hotel late Sunday afternoon and waved cheerily to the clerk as he walked through the lobby.

He lay on his bed, stared at the ceiling, and considered his position. The police were by now combing Hafen's records. They'd focus on people who'd lost cases to him. Jack would soon become a person of interest. It was essential he complete his task before the police concentrated their efforts on him.

Next week he'd call Reverend Simons in New York.

After a routine day of work in the operating room on Monday, Jack rented a garage-sized storage area in a facility guarded by electronic surveillance and limited access. On Tuesday he rented a van and purchased fifty storage boxes. He began packing and ferrying his personal property to the storage area. This occupied him for the next three evenings.

The first items taken to the facility were his personal firearms. He had the .22 caliber bolt-action rifle his father had given him on his fourteenth birthday, a 12-gauge pump shotgun he'd bought at age sixteen with money he'd earned baling hay, and a .270 caliber rifle he'd used on half a dozen big-game hunts in the Rocky Mountains. All the weapons had sentimental value. He transported each weapon in a hard case. In a carefully labeled storage box he placed the few boxes of leftover ammunition he possessed and his gun-cleaning gear. He packed with the care of a man who knew strangers would soon be examining his possessions.

Three evenings later he surveyed the room containing his worldly goods. Everything was stacked neatly and labeled clearly. Plenty of room for the BMW remained. He was satisfied.

He expected homicide detectives to interview him soon. Those guys were cynical and hard to fool. He had to steel himself. If he felt any doubt about the righteousness of his actions, any doubt at all, the detectives would trip him up. Then they'd take him, and if they took him, there'd be no justice. Dr. Jack Andrews had given up his career, his children, his wealth. For all that he must have justice.

Two days went by. Nobody called. He concluded it was going to take a little longer for the police to go through all the records and do the necessary background checks.

It looked like he was going to get the time he needed.

CHAPTER FIFTY-FOUR

Monday morning he made the call. "Fred, this is Jack. I wonder if I could come to New York and speak to you. I'm committed to becoming a missionary physician. I really intend to do this."

"Jack, I had my credentialing assistant go through your entire résumé, and also specifically investigate the malpractice case you lost. He believes one poor outcome doesn't prove a physician actually committed malpractice, nor does it disqualify a physician with an otherwise good record from being credentialed. He felt you were fully qualified for one of our locations in Africa. This clinic has two registered nurses but no MD's. It's becoming increasingly difficult to find medical personnel willing to work in an area where sixty or seventy percent of the population is HIV positive."

"Fred, just give me a chance."

The reverend sounded uneasy. "Jack, I have to evaluate people before placing them in difficult situations. The church has limited funds and can't afford expensive mistakes. We can't have a runner. Someone who's avoiding problems in his own life, someone who might change his mind after three months and demand an airline ticket home. I have to have a solid commitment for three years. After that time you can come back to the States for six months...There's so much need there, so many people depending on you. I have to know you're deeply committed. That you believe this mission is important to you. It's got to be more important to you than anything else."

"Fred, you know me. I've given you my word. If you give me a chance to serve I'll regard it as a privilege. I won't let you down."

"OK, Jack. How soon can we meet?"

"I can be there Friday."

"That's not much time for you to arrange a trip to New York. But if you can make it, I'm available. Bring your current hospital privileges and recent continuing medical education credits with you. We have that African clinic in desperate need of a physician. We'll streamline the process as much as we can. Your passport is in order, right?"

"The passport's current. How soon can I go?"

"There're always delays in credentialing overseas. But with the medical situation in the host country this extreme, I'm hoping we can grant you privileges within two months."

"I'm set. I'll give my notice of resignation to the hospital here immediately. I'll be ready to depart whenever the paperwork is complete."

"That's unusually fast. How can you be ready so soon?"

"I've been through with my life here for a long time, been preparing to leave for months. Delay won't help me in any way."

"Then we'll meet in my office Friday. Say, nine o'clock?"

"I'll be there."

CHAPTER FIFTY-FIVE

Jack went to the hospital credentialing office after concluding his call with Rev. Simons. He dictated identical letters of resignation to the president of the medical staff and the chair of the anesthesia group. To the secretary he said, "Would you mind typing the letters I've just dictated? I need them immediately. I'd like to sign and submit them before the close of business today."

The secretary, a self-important veteran of twenty years in the same job, declared, "Can't you see how busy I am? I'll probably get to your letters in a day or two."

Jack smiled and replied, "Really? How about this? Since each letter is just one sentence long, I'll just stay here until you can squeeze me into your busy schedule."

The secretary huffed. "Suit yourself." She retreated into a back office and shut the door.

Forty-five minutes later Richard Madison strode purposefully into the office, looking ridiculous in his expensive suit. Jack considered the juxtaposition of pomposity and incompetence. With amusement in his voice he said, "Dr. Madison, you aren't dressed in scrubs. Didn't anyone require your special talents today?"

Madison sneered, "Dr. Andrews, I see even losing a malpractice case hasn't diminished your predilection for making inappropriate comments. I'm here in my capacity as chair of the credentialing committee in regard to your letter of resignation from the medical staff."

"Wow. The letters haven't even been typed yet and you're already here. I'm amazed you have time to personally see to this, what with your busy schedule of performing anesthetics for easy operations on perfectly healthy, fully insured patients. This must be my lucky day."

"I've spoken with the members of the credentialing committee and the chief of the anesthesia department," Madison growled. "You won't be required to give a thirty-day notice prior to your resignation. In fact, you'll incur no penalty if you depart immediately upon signing the appropriate letters."

Jack laughed. "That's OK with me. But if I do that, I expect to receive my termination pay in a lump sum...tomorrow."

Madison became impatient. "I'll see to it myself. You'll receive an electronic transfer of funds tomorrow."

"How nice of you. Make sure it's in the right amount...You know, after I leave, the anesthesia department will be short of personnel. They may even have to call you at night to do an emergency heart operation or some terrible trauma. You'll have to pretend you're a real doctor. Think you're up to it?"

Madison turned on his heel and stalked out of the office. Jack called after him, "I don't think so either."

Jack returned to his hotel and spoke with the clerk. He'd be departing the next day and wished to settle his bill. He spent the afternoon moving his few remaining clothes, books, and papers to the storage facility. This required a taxi. He paid the manager of the facility one year's rent in advance. When he returned to the hotel room, it contained only the clothes he needed for the trip to New York. Everything left would fit into the touring cases of the BMW.

That evening, Jack called his daughters and arranged to take them out for pizza. He admitted it was unusual to meet on a weeknight, but insisted they spend an hour with him. Their resentment at the short notice was palpable in the taxi, and no one spoke until they were seated at a booth. He told them he'd accepted a new job and had to leave Omaha for an extended period of time. He promised to write and told them he would always love them. The girls pointed out they had to get home because they both had homework. After all, they always fulfilled their responsibilities.

Jack dropped them off and watched as they entered their house. He was certain nothing could alter his relationship with his daughters—not his presence nor his absence nor anything else.

CHAPTER FIFTY-SIX

Tuesday morning Jack went to his bank, confirmed the electronic deposit of his remaining pay, and withdrew five thousand dollars in cash. By eleven o'clock he was riding his bike east on the I-80. In perfect fall weather he passed through the congestion of Chicago and the blight of Gary, Indiana. He stopped long after dark at a motel in South Bend, Indiana, and slept not far from the University of Notre Dame.

On Wednesday he rode across the enormous croplands of Indiana and western Ohio and entered the great forests extending from eastern Ohio into Pennsylvania. Jack, a Midwesterner all his life, was amazed such lands still existed in the densely populated eastern part of his country. At dusk he exited north off I-80 and rode five miles to a small-town motel. He ate a burger in a café next door, returned to his room, and fell into an exhausted sleep.

Thursday morning after breakfast he rode on into the village and located a small hardware store. He parked the BMW two blocks down the street and packed his leathers and helmet away. Wearing jeans and a sweatshirt, he walked into the store and purchased an ax handle and a small handsaw. He paid cash and walked out with his tools in a large brown paper bag. On his way to the town park, Jack stopped at a food store and picked up a cup of hot chocolate and two doughnuts to go. He dropped the white bag with the doughnuts into the larger brown bag and ambled the four blocks to the park, sipping the hot chocolate. When he reached the park he sat at a picnic table and slowly ate the doughnuts and finished his drink.

He walked to a small grove of evergreen trees and looked around to ensure he wasn't under observation. As summer vacation was over,

189

the village's children were back in school and their parents were busy earning their living. Jack slipped into a spot surrounded by low-laying evergreen boughs, sat down, and fashioned the tool he needed. It took only a couple of minutes to saw the ax handle into two parts. The part he wanted was about a foot and a half long, and he pushed it into the white paper bag. The remainder of the ax handle and the saw he dropped back into the hardware store bag. Jack walked to a Dumpster full of debris from last weekend's picnics and pushed the brown bag down into the smelly, wet garbage.

He walked back to his bike, opened the top case, and put the white paper bag inside. He dressed in his leathers, pushed his helmet on, and brought the dark visor down. The BMW left the village quietly, ridden by a man who didn't present his face to the world. A predator on the prowl.

CHAPTER FIFTY-SEVEN

He arrived in New York City Thursday evening, found a hotel room, and, astounded by the price, paid cash for three nights' lodging. He ate at a nearby delicatessen and returned to his room. The next morning he rose, cleaned up, and dressed in trousers, a white shirt, and a sports jacket. These were advertised to remain wrinkle-free for the convenience of the frequent traveler, and, in truth, they were surprisingly presentable considering they'd been stuffed into a motorcycle touring case for the last few days. Jack took a cab to the building that housed Reverend Simons's sixth-floor office. The secretary welcomed him when he entered at 8:30 a.m. and offered him a cup of coffee. He accepted it and sat down with a magazine.

Simons arrived at ten minutes before nine. He wore black slacks, a black shirt with his clerical collar in place, and a black suit jacket. The reverend, a trim man six feet tall, walked with a decided limp, his left leg completely stiff. His neck was rigid, and he could turn his head only a few degrees. His formerly jet-black hair had turned steel gray. Here was a man who'd been grievously injured.

Jack looked into his friend's eyes. Reverend Simons radiated serenity. His shattered body couldn't hide his passion, competence and authority. He believed in his mission, and he lived life well.

Simons walked straight to his guest and offered his hand. "Welcome, Jack. It's great to see you again after all these years."

Jack was smiling, something that didn't come easily to him anymore. "Fred, thanks for allowing me to come."

The two men went into an office just off the reception area. The inexpensive desk and chairs demonstrated this mission society was dedicated to helping people. Its director didn't care about impressing donors or granting perks to his executives. There were no egotistical pictures or certificates on the walls. This was the working office of a committed believer.

Two old overstuffed chairs sat in front of the desk. Simons sat in one of them and indicated Jack should take the other. No desk or other prop separated the men.

"Jack, as we've discussed, there's a mission in East Africa in desperate need of a physician. Conditions there aren't good. The roads are so bad it'll take you ten hours to travel the one hundred miles from the nearest airport to the clinic. And that's if everything goes well. You know, no flat tires, broken axles, or holdups by the local bandits. This village is truly third world. You'll get enough to eat, but your diet won't be long on meat. In fact, any day you get anything to eat other than vegetables and grain will be a real treat. If you drink the local water you'll get sick. You'll have to take precautions and gradually acclimate to it. We send bottled water, but there's never enough of that. Your only entertainment will be the radio and the books you receive by mail. Need I mention the mail service is less than dependable? The clinic is primitive and there'll never be all the medicine or instruments you're accustomed to using. We're asking for a three-year commitment. That will earn you two months of vacation for every twelve months completed. For all this we pay you thirty-six thousand dollars a year and give you a round-trip ticket to New York every three years."

"Fred, how many patients will I see there?"

"You'll never be out of sight of people in desperate need of help. Most of them will be grateful and treat you with respect. But this is Africa, and there is really no government or police in the bush. The security an American expects as a birthright doesn't exist. I can't guarantee your safety."

"Fred, the life I've led has been all about money. Everyone—the physicians, the hospitals, and the lawyers who prey on them—is grasping for money. It's the only way they keep score. I need to find out if there's a better way to live life. I want to be a physician. I don't want to spend any more time evaluating my financial net worth. I'll try to live one day at a time and not think about anything except the welfare of my patients. You have my word. I'll stay three years and do my best every day."

There followed an hour's conversation concerning logistics. In six weeks he'd receive a plane ticket from Omaha to New York. After reaching New York, Jack planned to spend three days in consultation with the mission board. And then he'd depart for his new life in Africa.

Fred concluded, "Jack, I wish I could spend the weekend with you, but, regrettably, I have to honor a last-minute request to attend a fund-raiser in California. It's important, speaking to potential donors."

Jack replied, "That's OK. I need a couple days' rest anyway. Maybe I'll spend a little time investigating the big city. A Midwestern farm boy like me doesn't get many opportunities to take all this in. Then it's back to Omaha to tie up a few things before I leave."

Jack walked all the way back to his hotel. The walk cleared his mind. There really was only one errand to complete before beginning his new life. One last thing.

He laughed to himself. Closure was so important.

CHAPTER FIFTY-EIGHT

Early Saturday morning Jack departed for Chicago. Because he was leaving a day earlier than planned, he asked the hotel for the refund of one night's stay. The hotel, not surprisingly, refused.

He pushed hard on the road, stopping when necessary for gas or food. Twice he pulled into interstate rest areas, stretched out on the grass, and slept for two or three hours. Arriving in Chicago late Sunday evening, he found a hotel near O'Hare airport and paid cash for three nights' lodging.

The next morning he bought a Chicago Traveler's Guide at the hotel convenience store. The book included a detailed city map. One location interested Jack—a county hospital affiliated with the University of Illinois Medical School. Dr. Charles Kessler's advertisement in a legal journal specified this as his practice location. It also stressed his adjunct faculty position with the University of Illinois.

Jack studied the map. He had to know every way in and out of the killing ground. The terrain must not surprise him.

The motorcycle ride to the hospital on Monday evening took an hour and fifteen minutes. He left the BMW in a parking lot three blocks from the hospital's emergency room entrance and began a leisurely walk to familiarize himself with the surroundings. The hospital had probably been elegant once. Now it was a dirty brown building in a dirty brown section of town. Brightly lit signs indicated the location of the emergency room, ambulance parking, visitor parking, and main entrance. Someone had attempted some landscaping, even planting a few flowerbeds. All efforts to create a tiny green area in front of the brown building had been defeated by the crush of people and the garbage they deposited.

This was a charity hospital, a place where problem members of society came for free medical care administered by harried, incompletely trained resident physicians. Usually there was little supervision from the resident's faculty advisors. A faculty advisor with a second job, perhaps making money whoring for lawyers, could probably stay in his office all day. Such an advisor likely had little to do with patients or residents. He could take a few phone calls from residents and offer some off-the-cuff advice. He might even stroll over to the operating room to make an appearance. But nothing occurring in this hospital would ever interfere with his second, more remunerative career.

In truth, Dr. Charles Kessler only needed his faculty appointment to grant him legitimacy in a court of law. And the courtroom was the only place he was granted legitimacy. No one who understood medicine held him in high regard. Of course, people who understood medicine were ineligible for placement on a jury judging a doctor accused of malpractice.

Jack walked into the hospital's main entrance and located the admissions desk, the financial counselor's office, the cafeteria, and the information desk. Four banks of elevators were located at the back of the lobby, next to a directory. The operating rooms were on the second floor. It was probable they were directly above the emergency room. The offices of the Department of Anesthesia were located on the third floor. Dr. Charles Kessler, adjunct professor and chief of anesthesia, occupied room 3010.

No one was waiting for the elevator. Jack entered and pushed the button for the third floor. He noted the second floor button had a sign above it: OPERATING ROOM—LIMITED ACCESS. He walked off the elevator with the assurance of someone who worked on the third floor. Halfway down the hall on his right was a large glass door proclaiming DEPARTMENT OF ANESTHESIA. The office was dimly lit, as was expected at nine o'clock at night. Behind the door a reception desk blocked entry into the faculty offices. Three chairs and a magazine rack faced the desk. A forlorn artificial tree stood in the corner.

He continued walking down the corridor, past two restrooms and a door that said MAINTENANCE. He came to a T-intersection. A sign indicated the Department of Pathology was to the left and the Nursing Department to the right. He turned around in the empty hallway and walked past the Department of Anesthesia offices one more time. Straight ahead and twenty feet past the elevator door, the corridor ended with an exit sign over a door to a stairwell. Another sign advised people to utilize the stairwell in case of fire.

Jack took the stairs down to the first floor, exited the hospital through the lobby, walked to his bike, and rode leisurely back to the hotel. He entered his room, walked to the window, and stared at the bright lights of Chicago. He thought about closure.

CHAPTER FIFTY-NINE

Tuesday at 8:30 a.m. Jack used a throwaway cell phone to call the Department of Anesthesia. He identified himself as a sales representative for a well-known pharmaceutical company and said, "I'd like to speak with Professor Charles Kessler regarding a research project. My company is planning to market a new anesthesia agent and we need to conduct a study in an academic institution to demonstrate this agent's versatility and safety. This will be an extremely well funded project. Dr. Kessler comes highly recommended. Would it be possible for me to make an appointment with Dr. Kessler to discuss this matter?"

The secretary said, "I know Dr. Kessler will want to discuss your proposal. Research funds are difficult to obtain these days and Dr. Kessler is always anxious to further medical science. Let's see, Dr. Kessler is fully booked today. He's on call all night tomorrow, Wednesday, so he won't even arrive at the hospital until 3:00 p.m. It's so nice that Dr. Kessler accepts a slot on the call schedule, being the chief of anesthesia and all. Of course, this means Dr. Kessler will be off duty Thursday. Post-call day, don't you know? But there are appointment times available on Friday."

"Darn. I'm tied up on Friday this week. I'll check my schedule for the next week and get back to you. Thanks for all your help."

Jack spent the rest of Tuesday preparing. He found a uniform store with a blue work jumpsuit his size. Next stop was a hardware store, where he obtained a few tools, a tool belt, and a pair of workman's gloves. A Walmart store yielded a box of Handi Wipes and ziplock bags. Finally, he shopped at a sporting goods store and purchased a large athletic bag and a Chicago Cubs baseball cap.

He returned to his hotel room and spent time wondering if Charles Kessler's life had been fulfilling. He'd been well rewarded financially and he lived well. But did he actually believe he could continue lying in courtrooms and remain personally untouchable? Did he believe the world was filled with helpless victims for him to destroy? Apparently he did. He was a businessman who'd discovered his niche and meant to exploit it. That is, he'd exploit his niche as long as he were granted that opportunity.

Wednesday morning, Jack checked out of his hotel and rode downtown to a parking garage. He paid eighty dollars to park overnight. With his athletic bag slung over his shoulder he walked forty-five minutes, and then hailed a cab. A mile from his target's hospital he exited the cab and began walking in a leisurely manner. He stopped at a delicatessen at 2:30 p.m. and slowly washed down a sandwich with a Coke. He resumed a roundabout path to the hospital, reviewing the terrain. It wouldn't do to arrive too soon.

Jack entered the hospital lobby at 6:45 p.m., and, keeping his head down, walked to the stairwell. Walking quietly up the stairs, he strained to hear other footfalls. There were none. He opened the door on the third floor with a hand covered by a handkerchief and peered around the corner. The hallway was deserted. He walked to the restroom, locked the door, and looked around. The room was typical of such places in an aging medical building—one toilet, one sink, a paper towel dispenser, and a wastebasket. Opening the bag, he took out the blue jumpsuit and pulled it over his jeans and T-shirt. Then he retrieved the tool belt, making sure the few tools it contained were fully secure. He tucked the ax handle into the hammer carrier. The last object he removed from the bag was the Cubs cap. He disconnected the athletic bag's strap from one of its rings, rolled the bag tightly, and secured it under the jumpsuit and against the small of his back by reattaching the strap to its ring and pulling tight. He zipped the jumpsuit, buckled on the tool belt, and pulled the cap low over his forehead.

He used a damp paper towel to wash surfaces he'd touched, pulled his work gloves on, and used a screwdriver to shatter the fluorescent light over the sink. Exiting the bathroom into an empty hallway, he wiped the doorknob with the damp towel, tossed the towel into the wastebasket, and allowed the door to close.

He walked down the empty hallway to the stairwell and went through the door. He stood just beyond the door, holding it ajar with his toe. If someone approached Jack on the stairwell he'd say he was on his way to check out a complaint of a broken light bulb in the men's room.

His senses were alert, his mind empty. The details of the kill were fluid. The kill was a certainty. The predator awaited his prey.

At 7:50 p.m. the elevator bell sounded and a young man and a young woman, both dressed in short white jackets reserved for medical students, left the elevator. They walked down the hallway away from Jack without noticing the slightly open door behind them. They turned left toward Pathology. No one else moved in the corridor. The workers in these offices were government employees and it was well after quitting time. At 8:10 p.m. the two medical students, still uninterested in their immediate environment, returned to the elevator and departed.

At 8:55 p.m. Jack heard the elevator bell again, and Dr. Charles Kessler walked into the hallway alone. He wore a scrub suit covered by a surgical gown worn backward so the snaps were in the front. The gown was open. Dr. Kessler rotated a fanny pack forward and opened it as he walked to the anesthesia offices. He withdrew a key, signaling to Jack that no one was in the office to admit him.

Jack walked through the stairwell door, head down. He moved unhurriedly down the hall, avoiding eye contact. Dr. Kessler heard Jack's footsteps, looked up, and identified him as a janitorial or maintenance man, someone unworthy of a second look. He shoved the key into the lock and turned it. He was pushing the door open as Jack approached within six feet. He didn't look up until he realized the nonentity had suddenly moved in immediately behind him.

Charles Kessler began issuing a protest to this lout. Jack grabbed the back of Kessler's neck with his right hand and the door handle with his left. He opened the door wide and shoved the doctor forward and down. He wasn't gentle.

Kessler flew face first through the door and onto the floor. He looked up at the man standing over him and said indignantly, "How dare you."

Jack growled, "Not a word. If you make any noise I'll kill you." Kessler became nauseated and he urinated. "Stand up. We're going to your office. I require something you possess. Be smart and you'll get through this." Kessler slowly got up, turned, and staggered toward his office. He could feel the man's presence behind him.

They arrived at an office door: C. KESSLER, MD, CHIEF, ANESTHESIA. The doctor opened the door and entered. Jack followed and pushed the door shut with his foot. A computer screen dimly illuminated the room.

Still with his back to his assailant, Kessler reached into his fanny pack and slowly eased out a container of pepper spray. He was always prepared because he lived in a dangerous city and was an individual of superior intellect. He turned suddenly toward Jack, extending his right hand with the container toward him.

Jack stepped to the right, away from the spray. He raised the ax handle shoulder-high and brought it down on the doctor's left arm, striking just above the elbow. The humerus shattered. The pepper spray fell from Kessler's right hand and clattered to the floor.

The ax handle completed its arc downward. When it reached the full extent of Jack's reach he took a half step to his left with his right foot to turn his body just enough. "Remember me? I'm Jack Andrews, the sap from Omaha whose career you ruined. And you did it for just a few thousand dollars." There was a flutter of recognition in the doctor's eyes.

Jack brought the ax handle up viciously. The weapon struck Kessler on the jaw, which fractured easier than his humerus had. He fell backward and lay on his back. His eyes were open. He moaned. Blood was everywhere. There was always a lot of hemorrhage with facial trauma.

Dr. Kessler's beeper went off. How unfortunate, Jack thought. He'd wanted to discuss the sin of greed with this self-proclaimed expert, but now someone was seeking the faculty anesthesiologist. Jack had no time for further consultation.

He turned Kessler over on his face and brought the ax handle down on the back of his head. He felt the skull crush. He brought the handle down twice more. The last time it felt as if he'd cracked a hard-boiled egg.

Jack bent over and wiped the ax handle thoroughly with Kessler's surgical gown, then secured it in his tool belt. He walked out of the office, out of the department complex, and went straight to the stairwell. He didn't look back.

Entering the stairwell, he stopped and listened for ten seconds. Nothing. He unzipped the jumpsuit, unfastened the athletic bag, and unrolled it at his feet. He dropped his gloves into the bag, followed by the tool belt, the Cubs hat, and the jumpsuit. He removed a ziplock bag of Handi Wipes from the back pocket of his jeans and wiped his face, neck, hands—anywhere he might have been splattered with blood. The Handi Wipes and the ziplock went into the bag. Then he closed the zipper, attached the carrying strap, and slung the bag over his shoulder.

He walked down the stairs to the first floor. Pushing the door release with the back of his right hand, he entered the lobby. Keeping his head down, he walked unhurriedly to the exit. There were no alarms. No one was rushing anywhere. The automatic doors opened and the night welcomed him.

After walking half an hour, he hailed a cab. The cab dropped him at a hotel within a block of the parking garage. He opened the top case, took out his leathers and helmet, and put the athletic bag into the now empty space. He dressed and began his trip west. Traffic surrounded him, but he felt invisible.

CHAPTER SIXTY

O ne hundred miles from Chicago Jack began thinking about the athletic bag. Initially he considered stopping the bike, extracting the evidence, and hurling it into a ditch. But he realized that, in medical parlance, such an act would constitute poor judgment. It would be unwise to leave the bag where a curious motorist might find it. The jumpsuit and the ax handle were stained with Charles Kessler's blood. Hair from Jack's body was certain to be somewhere in the jumpsuit and cap. DNA analysis is precise. The evidence had to be burned.

I-80 took him straight west. He traveled for eight hours, stopping twice for gas, candy, and caffeine. The solution dawned on him.

Just east of Des Moines Jack exited north off I-80 and headed for a spot forty-five minutes away. His home farm could serve him one last time. The farm had been sold to a second cousin after it became apparent that neither Jack nor his siblings were interested in the rural lifestyle and its insecurities. The cousin had bulldozed the decrepit farm buildings, which were all of them. But, with sentimentality unusual in the agricultural world, he'd allowed a small grove of trees to remain. It would be good to see the old place one more time.

Thirty miles off the interstate Jack stopped at a familiar store, a place that sold saddles, bridles, and other tack for horse enthusiasts. It also sold western clothing. The storeowner had long ago attended Jack's high school football games. He'd conducted business with the Andrews family for years, and he greeted Jack warmly. "The doctor has come back to visit us after all these years. I still see your cousins and assorted relatives pretty regular, but I've missed visiting with you."

Jack smiled. "It's nice to see you again. I miss all my old friends. You know, I live in Omaha now, and I just can't seem to find good cowboy boots there. Thought I'd come to the world's best store and pick up some quality footwear."

"You've always had excellent taste, Jack. Our selection is pretty good, and I bet you'll find something you like."

Jack left the store half an hour later with a pair of dark brown cowboy boots, two pairs of boot-cut jeans, and a denim shirt.

Five miles down the road he stopped at a Casey's store, the convenience center of the small Midwestern town. He topped off his gas tank and bought a bottle of Coke and a package of hot dogs. No one recognized Jack in the store, and he recognized no one. It'd been a long time since he'd left his hometown.

Ten minutes later Jack rode up the gravel lane to his old homestead. It gratified him to see the old trees again, alive and unchanged after all these years. As he expected, no one was working the fields. It wasn't quite time to harvest the corn yet. After dropping his leathers and helmet next to his bike, he walked into the grove and found what he knew must be there. An old tree had fallen years before, littering the surrounding area with branches and sticks. Jack started a small fire, beginning with kindling and using increasingly larger branches to create a fire big enough to generate heat.

From the BMW he retrieved the athletic bag. Back at the fire, he fed the flames with the ax handle, the jumpsuit, the gloves, the tool belt, the Cubs hat, and finally the athletic bag itself. He went back to the bike and retrieved underwear, socks, and his new western attire. All the clothes he'd worn in Chicago, including his riding boots, he burned.

He spent the next hour feeding the fire dry branches, making sure the flames didn't become too large and noticeable. Still alone, he spitted two hot dogs, cooked them over the flame, ate, and then sat a long time studying the coals. The flames dropped and the fire turned blue. Jack threw the remaining hot dogs and the empty plastic Coke bottle into the flames. He watched the bottle melt and shrivel into nothingness.

Returning to the BMW, he opened his tool kit and removed all the components of the .45 and its ammunition. All the parts went into the front pockets of his leather jacket. When he left the farm after dark, he intended to distribute the ammunition and the separate parts of the pistol in gravel road ditches over a ten-mile area. The process would begin after he'd traveled more than five miles from the grove.

Jack walked back to the smoldering fire to make sure it couldn't spread. Half an hour after sunset he started his bike and said farewell to his boyhood home.

CHAPTER SIXTY-ONE

Well after midnight Jack checked back into his familiar hotel. He paid cash in advance for two weeks' lodging. "You sure have an unusual lifestyle," the clerk observed. "What's in store for you now?"

"I'm making a change in careers," Jack replied. "I have to tie up a few loose ends in Omaha, then I'm off on a two-week cross-country ride. Going to the Black Hills and Yellowstone and anywhere else west of here that strikes my fancy. After that I'll come back to Omaha to make sure my stuff is securely stored. I'll conclude my responsibilities and take off on a new career adventure." He took the room key and carried his clothing to his room. He slept off and on for fifteen hours.

He awoke with a start at five in the afternoon. The phone message light was blinking. Jack called the front desk and recognized the clerk's old-man voice. "Jack Andrews here. Room four seventeen. Is there a message for me?"

"Ah, yes, Dr. Andrews. A police officer called. Name of Michael Weber. He said he'd like to speak with you. Didn't say why."

"Thanks. I'll call him later."

Jack didn't return the call. It seemed strange not to. He'd always returned calls immediately, something necessary when you worked in the operating room. Problems were often urgent and needed to be addressed right now. But the OR's problems he'd addressed were always other people's problems—a surgeon's or maybe even a patient's. He decided to address his own problems cautiously and in his own good time.

He rolled out of bed, shaved, showered, and dressed. He carried all the clothes he wasn't wearing to the hotel laundromat to wash and dry. He finished at 8 p.m. and noticed he was hungry.

He walked to his favorite restaurant and ordered a T-bone steak. He was waiting for his meal when a man entered the room and drew Jack's attention. The man obviously cared about his appearance. He wore a tie, sport coat, and well-cut slacks. His shoes were polished. His hair was short and his moustache well groomed. His eyes expressed slight amusement as he looked over the patrons. He was making a statement. He was a cop. He was tough and he was smart. He didn't suffer fools lightly.

Michael Weber saw Dr. Jack Andrews looking directly at him. Andrews didn't cringe. He didn't look guilty. He looked attentive. Weber thought, *This guy's going to be interesting.*

He walked to Jack's table. "Dr. Andrews? I'm Sergeant Michael Weber from the homicide division. I've been anxious to meet you. Mind if I sit down?"

Jack indicated with his right hand, palm up, that Weber was welcome to sit in the chair opposite him. Jack's face and eyes were void of emotion. Weber thought, *I'll bet he handles problems in the operating room the same way. Emotion in that environment probably makes things worse.*

"Dr. Andrews, we meet at last. Addressing you as Doctor seems so stilted. Here we are, just two regular guys. Mind if I call you Jack?"

"Why not?" Jack said reasonably. "And I'll call you Mike, right?"

"You know, Jack, a lot of your acquaintances have turned up dead lately."

"Really? I don't know anything about that. But whoever died couldn't have been too close a friend. I haven't been invited to any funerals lately."

"You're a cute guy, Jack. Maybe you should get a lawyer and come downtown to talk to me."

"I don't need a lawyer, Mike. Lawyers are only for guilty guys. Or people planning to rip someone off."

"You remember Carl Hafen, Jack?"

"Of course. He's a hard guy to forget."

"Carl's dead. But you already know that. So are his secretary and her husband. Funny thing, the husband worked in an operating room, the same one you did. I understand he made some of the doctors uncomfortable."

"That's really awful, Mike."

"Some guy whacked them. A guy familiar with firearms."

"You guys ought to pick him up."

"Another thing, Jack. Ben Harris, your first attorney in your malpractice fiasco, turned up dead with what people thought was a heart attack. Maybe we should exhume him."

"Sounds like that'd be a smelly job."

"You're a cocky son of a bitch. I like that. It makes things so much more rewarding."

"Say, Mike, my steak's on the way. You should order something. My treat. I hate eating alone."

"You better enjoy your solitude. There's not much privacy in prison."

"Does that mean you aren't staying for dinner?"

Michael Weber stood up, his character assessment complete. "Don't worry, Doc. You'll be seeing a lot more of me in the future."

As Weber walked away Jack thought, *He hasn't heard about Kessler—yet.*

CHAPTER SIXTY-TWO

Jack called his divorce lawyer the next afternoon. "Hello, Jordan. Jack Andrews here. I'm making a career change. I'll be out of the country for the next three years. My annual income will be thirty-six grand. My child support payments need to be reevaluated."

There was a long pause. The lawyer, her voice incredulous, said, "Is this a joke?"

"Nope. I've given up private practice to become a medical missionary in Africa. I'm leaving in six weeks. By the way, you can tell Kate she can have the girls every Christmas from now on."

"You can't do that. The court will say you're avoiding your paternal responsibilities."

"You think the court will come down on me for dedicating my life to the welfare of humankind?"

"The court will say you can do any fool thing you want. Then they'll say those two girls are a doctor's kids. My opponent will demand you pay the set amount of child support from your remaining marital assets because you refuse to work and support the children in the manner they think they deserve."

"You know, Jordan, most of my assets already went to Kate. I'm afraid I've blown the rest on high living. I'll do this: I'll put one year's child support in the bank and order monthly payments be made to Kate. That way you have a whole year to get things straightened out. Estimate your bill for the whole process and I'll pay you before I leave. Tell Kate she can come to Africa if she wants to argue with me. Make sure to mention that two-thirds of the people in the province where I'll be working are HIV positive. Caution her to be careful when she

208

comes over. Wouldn't want her to get injured and require a blood transfusion."

"You're a bastard."

"Jordan, I don't think an officer of the court should talk like that. Anyway, better get anything requiring my signature done quickly. I'm leaving in six weeks."

As Jack hung up he mused, *She'll pursue justice right up to the last dollar of her retainer. Then she'll settle.*

CHAPTER SIXTY-THREE

That evening Jack considered phoning his daughters, but decided to avoid the confrontation. He'd wait a few days, get everything ready for departure, and then say goodbye. Nothing he did could make his children think less of him. Perhaps when he returned from Africa in three years they'd be willing to relate to him as their father. Now they just wanted a provider.

The rest of the evening he spent organizing personal details, especially bank arrangements.

His phone woke him at nine o'clock. Michael Weber sounded chipper. "Top of the morning, Doc. Bet you can't guess what I just discovered."

Jack could feel his heart pounding, but he kept his voice flat. "I haven't a clue, Mike. Enlighten me."

"We've been tracking your interactions with Hafen. You knew we'd be doing that. And we decided to talk to the expert witness who nailed you in the malpractice case. Charles Kessler. And guess what? He just got whacked. A really brutal, ugly job. Very, very personal. And, lo and behold, this happened when you were out of Omaha. What a coincidence, huh?"

"Am I supposed to express some degree of shock or regret?"

"No, Doc, I wouldn't expect that at all. I do think it would be an excellent idea if you came downtown. For a chat."

"Be glad to, Mike. What time is good for you?"

"One o'clock would be nice. My office is at police headquarters, three twenty-seven Maple."

"I'll be there."

"Better bring a lawyer, Doc."

"I'll be there alone."

Jack hung up. He stared straight ahead. Michael Weber knew he'd killed Carl Hafen, Charles Kessler, all the others. If Jack had somehow fucked up and left any incriminating evidence, he'd go down. If there was no evidence, Weber would try to get him to incriminate himself. He had to extract himself now that the hunt was over. Personal extraction is always the final maneuver when one chooses to hunt dangerous game.

CHAPTER SIXTY-FOUR

Upon his arrival at police headquarters, Jack was politely directed to Michael Weber's office. Weber was standing outside a door graced with a sign announcing his name and rank. He greeted Jack formally and indicated a conference room where the interview would take place. Jack walked in, Weber followed. A police officer in plain clothes stepped in behind them.

Weber said, "Dr. Andrews, this is Sergeant Lawrence Allen. He'll be staying for the interview."

Weber placed a recording device on the table, right in the middle. Then he and Allen sat in chairs directly across the table from Jack. Weber turned the recorder on. He identified himself, Allen, and Dr. Jack Andrews. He gave the place, date, and time. Then he looked directly at Jack.

"Dr. Andrews, this interview is part of a murder investigation. You are a suspect. I am informing you of this so you can, if you choose, retain an attorney. We will stop right now if you want an attorney present."

"I don't want an attorney. I'll answer your questions."

The two cops looked at each other, surprised. Weber said, "For the record, Doctor, you say you do not wish an attorney to be present?"

"I don't need an attorney." There was a palpable pause. "Am I being charged with a crime?"

"No, Doctor, we are engaged in a murder investigation. This is part of the process. Unless you'd like to make a confession."

Jack looked straight back at Weber.

"Doctor, I'll take your silence as an indication you don't feel compelled to confess. We're looking into the murder of Carl Hafen and the murders of his secretary and her husband. We believe these murders are connected. Hafen was pretty hard on you. Our investigation indicates your life has been in a tailspin since you tangled with him. You went through a bitter, expensive divorce. Your practice of anesthesiology has suffered. Lately, you've been earning less than half your former salary because, for whatever reason, you are unable or unwilling to work as hard as you did before. And now, in what some of your colleagues believe to be a fit of insanity, you've quit medicine altogether. Now, this all adds up to a real problem for you because a physician who quits his practice after a malpractice conviction will certainly have problems securing another position."

Jack replied quietly and with careful consideration. He sounded meticulous, not arrogant. "I think you'll find a lot of physicians have problems after being accused of malpractice. There are even suicides. In my own case I've decided to redirect my energies."

"You don't believe you were guilty of malpractice. That's correct, isn't it, Doctor?"

"I didn't commit malpractice."

"Well then, Doctor, how come a respected member of the medical establishment like Dr. Charles Kessler decided to testify against you?"

"Dr. Charles Kessler testifies for money."

"Testified, Doctor. Dr. Kessler is dead."

"So you told me on the phone."

"You didn't like him much, did you, Doctor?"

"Of course not. Would you?"

"I bet you wanted him dead."

"I only wanted him to tell the truth."

"You're quite good with firearms, aren't you, Doctor?"

"I'm competent."

"But you've hunted a lot of animals. You've even killed big game."

"I'm competent."

"What if we subpoenaed all the weapons you own? For ballistic tests."

"They're all in a storage facility. I'll give you the key right now."

"Do you own firearms other than those in the storage facility?"

"No."

"We can check the federal records for purchase of firearms."

"Go ahead."

"Is it coincidental that Charles Kessler died during the time you were absent from Omaha?"

"Must be."

"We discovered another point of interest. Your first lawyer in the malpractice case, Ben Harris, died recently too. He was another person who disappointed you. After all, you did fire him. What about that? Another coincidence?"

"Poor Ben Harris. He always appeared to be in fragile health."

The questioning went on for two hours. Jack couldn't remember where he'd been when all those murders took place. He'd never kept a daily log. He understood attorneys and expert witnesses were just doing their jobs. Jack had left the private practice of medicine because he was weary of talking to attorneys, administrators, insurance company clerks, and dissatisfied, whiny patients. He just wanted a life where he could serve people without constantly worrying about things he couldn't control. Sure, Jack missed his daughters, but it was an unhappy marriage, and perhaps it was best if they didn't have to witness the tension between his ex-wife and him. Money wasn't that important to him anymore. And finally, Jack recognized vengeance was only for fools. A desire for retribution could only result in his becoming an embittered man.

"What are you going to do, Doc?"

"I'm leaving in a few weeks for Africa. I'm going to be a medical missionary."

"Don't make me laugh."

"I'm serious."

"Trying to run away from me. It won't work."

"If you have evidence, charge me. But you better make it stick. If you take my last dream away from me and then can't prove I'm guilty—well, that's when I get a lawyer and come after the Omaha Police Department."

"We can extradite you from a foreign country."

"If you charge me, I'll come back on my own. I'll want to clear my name. That's all I have left."

Weber turned off the recorder. He indicated Sergeant Allen should leave the room. Allen closed the door as he left.

"You're going to Africa to do your penance, are you, Doc?"

"I don't have to offer penance."

"Doc, you're pretty cold. Did you leave your emotions in an operating room somewhere?"

Jack Andrews got up to leave. "Mike, I'm just a product of the system."

Acknowledgments

Thanks, Kasey, for guiding me through the publishing process. You did for your father what you do in your professional life-you solve problems. I also appreciate my friend, Tom Dollison, CRNA, for his expertise and unfailing good humor in directing my electronic communication, an area that continues to baffle me.

And thank you Patricia, my wife, for reading every version of this work over several years and contributing sage advice for its improvement. It means a lot to me that you believe I have something to say.

Made in the USA
San Bernardino, CA
30 September 2015